THE HAUNTED NORTHWOODS

THE HAUNTED NORTHWOODS

by TOM HOLLATZ
with Seal Dwyer

NORTH STAR PRESS OF ST. CLOUD, INC.

Printed in the United States of America by:
Versa Press, Inc.
East Peoria, IL 61611

Published by:
North Star Press of St. Cloud, Inc.
PO Box 451
St. Cloud MN 56302

Cover photos: Tom Hollatz

Cover design: Seal Dwyer

All photos, unless otherwise noted, are by Tom Hollatz.

ISBN: 0-87839-144-4

ACKNOWLEDGEMENTS

I wish to thank Lee Adams, Lynn Renor, Judy Olson, Tariq Eyssa, Ramy Renor, Julia McPeek, Julie Wood, Ginny St. Louis, Joe Simonton, Diana Anderson, Susan Lampert Smith, Donna Weikert, Dennis Boyer, Rich Rouse, Louella Doss, Hill Graywin, Marlene Voll, Virgil Beck, Ron Eckstein, James Seal, Lisa Lombardi-Rice, William P. Rice, Anne Keegan, Nick VanderPuy, Ken Kuttunen, Muffy, Pamela Jekel, Ann Wittman, Lori, Kathi Bertolino, Lee Davis, Art Hellyer, Jean Feraca, Jim Packard, Mark Hartzheim, Scott Simon, Michael Guilleb, Ami Tan, Kathy Olson, Sue Hanrahan, Russ and Pat Rydin, Dan Mosay, Steve Moe, Marcy Chuckel, Beth Gauper, Lady Catherine, Jeanine Sill, George Friedrich, Bruce Beckman, Sven, Franz Perfect, Ray Smallish, Jr., Joe Lisner, Eddie the Woofer, Peg Beitzel, Josephine, Walter Andrus, Guy Collins, Lori Roberts, Joe Drewniak, Bruce Wilsie, Paul Eck, Earl Einer, Bob Witkowski, Barbara Hill, Tracey Cejda, Kris Wiltzius, Dominic Paptola, Marshal Lewis, Phil Barnard, Frank and Margaret Maciejewski, Larry Meiller, Joanne Ohlsson, Paul F. Boller, Jr., Richard Crowe, Robert Bushman, Jeff Rovin, Joan "Cissy" Krynicki, Jody Kennedy, Emily Forsythe Warrne, Anne Llewellyn Barstow, Luigi Mendicino, and Porter "Barefoot" Dean.

TABLE OF CONTENTS

Introduction 1
Part One: The Summerwind Saga 3
    The Summerwind Legend 4
Part Two: Other Tales 36
    The Paulding Lights 37
    The Tale of Tobie 53
    The Mystery of Trout Lake 58
    The Scott Mansion of Merrill, Wisconsin 60
    Lori's Tale 64
    Werewolf in Wisconsin? 67
    Strange Noises in Oak Park 69
    Halloween On-Air 71
    Through A Child's Eyes 74
    Ghostly Visitors and Eerie Charm 76
    Minnesota Town Full of Haunts 78
    Lady Catherine's Strange Encounter 89

A Strangeness at Book World in Hayward 91

Josie of Eagle River and Other Tales 93

Art Hellyer Sees Something Strange 96

The Hurley Mystery of Lotta Morgan 99

Gangsters 102

UFO Sightings 105

The House in Ontonogon 108

Roscoe the Playful Poltergeist 112

The Stevenson Creek Chimney Mystery 118

"As a pale phantom with a lamp
Ascends some ruin's haunted stair,
So glides the moon along the damp
Mysterious chambers of the air.

Now hidden in cloud, and now revealed,
As if this phantom, full of pain,
Were by crumbling walls concealed,
And at the windows seen again."

Henry Wadsworth Longfellow
(1807-1882)
from "Moonlight"

INTRODUCTION

The cool damp of the deep Northwoods holds mysteries in the quiet twilight. When walking in such a woods, and upon stepping into a clearing where dust motes are circling through beams of sunshine and a tiny brook is bubbling over moss-covered stones, it always seems that the human footstep is the alien one. The gentle scene playing out in the clearing is frozen as the players wait for the intruder to pass.

It is just as easy to imagine all manner of ghosts and spirits among the dark boughs of the evergreens and the mid-summer shimmer of the aspens, playing in these most quiet of places as they did in life. In this land of crystal lakes and brooks, rustling leaves, and chattering animals, spirits live eternity in a paradise not unlike the one that they once knew.

As humans intrude upon the silence and peace of the area, sometimes they cannot help but come in contact with these other worlds. Some humans even seek them out and visit them with persistent regularity.

Ghost stories carry with them, as a matter of course, a glimpse into these worlds and the tales of those who ventured close to the border between our worlds. Some tales are looked upon with wonder at the histories that assert themselves around the edges. Some are to be feared as the fragments of childhood terrors, bound from consciousness by age, leap forth from dark corners of closets and beneath beds.

Skeptics claim that there are no ghosts, simply the fears of the gullible. Imagination running amuck with wits. However, it would seem that these people must not have felt the cold grasp of a dead child upon their shoulder in the dead of the night. Perhaps these people have not wandered down a lonely road and looked up to see a girl in a long white gown float across the road.

For those who have seen, felt or heard ghosts, there can be no doubt in their minds of what they experienced. There is a sense of connectedness in relating these stories to others. A sense that we are not alone.

The Northwoods of Wisconsin, Minnesota, and Michigan has a deep, rich history that lends itself to ghostly influence. Stories seem to sprout from the pine-needle-covered forest floor.

In this collection of ghost stories, each told in such a way as to captivate readers of all ages, there is a constant sense of the mysteries that pervades these *Haunted Northwoods*.

PART ONE

THE SUMMERWIND SAGA

THE SUMMERWIND LEGEND

Sometimes a single event is enough to fuel obsession. While reading a magazine one morning at my rural Boulder Junction, Wisconsin, home, I came across an article discussing haunted houses, one of which was just north of my home, Bear Lodge. The article wound its way through the complex and tragic history of the place. There was just enough written, and left unwritten, to send me on a secret quest to discover as much as I could about a place called Summerwind.

The article had not specified where Summerwind sat, only that it was on the shore of a northern Wisconsin lake. Since there are so many lakes in northern Wisconsin, I knew it was a hopeless case to go charging off in search of a certain run-down old building on the shores of a certain lake. However, questions continued to nag at me.

Spurred by the morsels of history in the article, I set off in search of any information I could find on Summerwind. The more I searched, the more questions seemed to conjure themselves in my head. There were some things that just

The road to Summerwind is always fascinating. No matter how many times I've been there—at least fifty—I always miss the right road.

did not add up to a ghost story. Perhaps the indisputable fact is not really possible and to create a good tale, details must be brought in and used whether they are possible or not. The legends of Summerwind are like this. The tales are good but sometimes, they don't stand up to close scrutiny, even if they are great with s'mores around the campfire.

Legends of Summerwind swirl through the history of northern Wisconsin like the winds off West Bay Lake that flow through the windows jams of the area—following no particular pattern but blowing strongly. Goaded by the tales of the people who had visited the place and by several books that told of marvelous things, the legends have risen to almost fever-pitch in the past several years. Perhaps one of the most famous of the legends of Summerwind concerns the ghost of an English explorer named Jonathan Carver. According to a book published in 1979, Carver haunts Summerwind in a attempt to find the deed to his Wisconsin properties. Carver was a well-known English explorer; purportedly he even met Benjamin Franklin in London in the spring of 1769.

Many things about the life of Jonathan Carver are uncertain and muddled by time and obscurity. Carver was heavily involved in the French and Indian Wars. He joined the militia in 1755 at the age of forty-five, mustering out eight years later at the age of fifty-three. He was then hired to go west into the uncharted wilderness and create maps and surveys that could be used for incoming settlers. He spent three years moving west to find the fabled "Northwest Passage," a water route across the continent to the Pacific Ocean. Carver spent a great deal of time among the Native Americans whom he came across on his travels. He also spent many months in the army post now known as Mackinac, Michigan. His journal of the trip, called the *Travels through the Interior Parts of North America in the Years 1766, 1767, 1768*, was published, after glitches and financial trouble, in 1778. The book was instantly snapped up by the upper-crust of European society and was received well, becoming the most widely read exploration book of its time. However, there were many faults in the book, and many of the stories were said to have been plagerized from other explorers' tales. Until the original journals were found in the British Museum in the early part of the 1900s, it was thought that Carver had written the contested material. However, the journals proved that Carver had not written the stories; they had been padded by his overzealous editor. On the other hand, some modern historians have conceded that Carver's journals are clean of any tampering or untruth.

A second book, *The Journals of Jonathan Carver and Related Documents, 1766-1770*, edited by John Parker, was first published in London, by a Dr. Lettsom, as a collection of Carver's papers. This book was reprinted by the

Minnesota Historical Society. It contained much information and papers written by Carver, but the famed deed forming the basis of the many legends was not included in the original publication of the book. The deed was printed in the book's second edition, supposedly after the death of Carver's wife, who had custody of it until then.

The deed's very existence is in question. There were several editions of *The Journals of Jonathan Carver and Related Documents, 1766-1770* published. Because Lettsom added the text of the deed for his second and subsequent editions, questions have proliferated regarding the validity of the deed itself. That, in and of itself, is enough for historians to doubt the existence of the deed. Some have gone so far as to call it "fraudulent."

The deed was reportedly drafted and signed on May 1, 1767. A council was held in a great cave, now known as Carver's Cave, under the bluffs of the Mississippi River near St. Paul, Minnesota. This council, according to *The Journals,* drafted a document that gave much of present-day Wisconsin and part of eastern Minnesota to Jonathan Carver "in return for the many presents, and further good services." The parcel that was given to Carver was "a tract of land that stretched from the Falls of St. Anthony along the east side of the Mississippi River south to the mouth of the Chippewa River, then due east for 100 miles, due north for 120 miles, and back in a straight line to the Falls of St. Anthony. It included what is now the west-central portion of Wisconsin and the southeastern corner of Minnesota, encompassing the site of present St. Paul."

The deed was signed by Hawnopawjatin and Otohtongoomlisheaw, two names mentioned as belonging to two Sioux chiefs whom Carver had known. Dr. Lettsom apparently gave the deed to Carver's widow, who was living in London at the time. After her death, he sought to locate it but without success, and in 1804 he concluded that it no longer existed. How he had received custody of it in the first place remains a mystery.

While Lettsom included this deed in his second edition text of the *Journals*, there is no mention of such an event in Carver's *Travels*. *Travels* mentions the cave and gives great detail about the majesty of this natural phenomenon and the petroglyphs on the soft sandstone walls of the cave. Logic tends to follow that, since Carver was meticulous in mentioning every detail he encountered on his journey, it seems that he would have at least hinted as to a deed that gave him a parcel of land the size of Wisconsin.

Countering that is the curious fact that when the West was being settled and great swaths of land were being claimed for one nation or another, the land contained in Carver's deed was never claimed, nor was it contested. The land in question was a lush area filled with natural resources and wildlife; it is very curious that it was not claimed and carved up like the rest of the continent.

The legend states that the deed is at Summerwind, sealed in a box buried in the foundation. However, the deed, which somehow found its way into the hands of Dr. Lettsom and then the wife of Carver, was last seen in London. Carver, himself, after his expedition, went to London to see about the publication of his book. Even though his book received incredible acclaim, it came far too late for Carver to enjoy the benefits. He died, destitute, in 1780 and was buried in a potter's field in London.

After Lettsom had given up his search for the the deed in 1804, Samuel Harrison of Chittenden, Vermont, who was related by marriage to one of Jonathan Carver's American granddaughters, took it upon himself to establish the rights of Carver's heirs to the land grant. He wrote to the Rev. Samuel Peters, a fellow New Englander who was then living in London, and asked him to take up the search for the original deed. Peters, a seventy-year-old former Episcopal minister, was a fervent loyalist who had been forced to leave his native Connecticut in 1774 as a result of his political opinions. In 1804, when he received Harrison's letter, he was living without income, and the Carver grant probably looked like a pot of gold capable of pulling him from the pits of poverty and ruin. He promptly embarked on a twenty-year quest for the validation of the grant. After years of rifling through papers, sifting through rumors and conjecture and going through legal channels, his work ended with no leads and no more money than the trifles with which he had begun. Despite his efforts, the deed was never granted validation by the United States Congress, nor by anyone else. Like many other treaties at the time, it was given little credence and fell by the wayside. The fact that there was no physical proof, other than the copy in the *Journals*, did not help. Many people regarded the heirs of Carver as liars, trying to create some benefit for themselves from the shreds that were left to them by their progeny.

During the latter half of 1832, German Prince Maximilian of Wied-Neuwied toured the wild interior of North America to study the Plains Indian people. Stories of the American West had thrilled the hearts of the royal heads and prominent leaders of Europe. Everything from the buffalo hunts to the Native Americans became stylish and much studied in the courts of Europe. Among the intrigued, Maximilian and hordes of other Europeans and East Coast Americans ventured into the untamed lands in the same numbers that were setting off for Africa for safari at the end of the century. Maximilian feasted on the early adventurers' and explorers' reports. Each person who penetrated this "untouched" land became an instant hero to these people. Meriwether Lewis and William Clark, Zebulon Pike, and explorer Jonathan Carver received acclaim akin to that of Hollywood stars in modern times. And, though not all the men who took up these quests are

remembered today, Carver's involvement in the early fab-
ric of this country is evident. His contributions are honored
in the naming of several counties, cities, and natural phenomenon in the Midwest.

Carver's deed was not given any credence and was
basically ignored, leaving the land to be divided later at the
whims of the settlers who moved in after the land had been
tamed somewhat and the eastern states had become so full
that to find land for new farms was becoming difficult. Of
the rest of Carver's life, not that much is known. His death
was anything but spectacular.

Summerwind was built in 1916 by a man named Robert
Patterson Lamont, who was later the United States Secretary
of Commerce under President Herbert Hoover. Lamont,
who was known to the public as a personable man, hailed
from Chicago, but his love was for the deep woods of northern Wisconsin. Some claimed that it was the natural air con-
ditioning that drew him, especially when the Chicago sum-

In 1925, the Summerwind mansion was one of the great showplaces in the wilds of the
Northwoods. Located on a hill, the mansion offered an exquisite view of West Bay Lake in
Land O' Lakes, Wisconsin. (Photo courtesy Bent's Camp.)

mers made the wool suits and celluloid collars, the uniform of the professional class, seem more like personal saunas.

According to one story, Lamont designed Summerwind as an escape for himself and his wife, a haven of calm away from the roiling mish-mash of people and politics in New York, Washington, and Chicago. Together, they lovingly filled it with antiques purchased during the course of numerous trips abroad. The tales of the items that filled Summerwind are enough to set almost any collector salivating. Of great note was a pool table that graced the basement of the building. It held its place in state and was used with great regularity.

Lamont was known to have seen ghosts in Summerwind, even then. Legend has it that there were several bullet holes in the basement door. Supposedly, Lamont shot them while in his kitchen, protecting himself from the ghosts that plagued him.

The ghost of Jonathan Carver did not enter the legend of Summerwind until 1979, when Wolfgang van Bober, aka Raymond Bober, wrote a book called the *Carver Effect*, naming Jonathan Carver as the identity of the ghost. Bober's daughter had lived in the house for about six months, during which time horrid things happened to her family. Among them, a corpse was found in a secret cubby-hole in a closet; the husband, who played an organ, would bang away at the keys until early morning, claiming the ghosts made him do it; gunshots were heard, but the only holes found were the ones that were rounded with age — the ones made by Lamont fifty years before — and the kitchen was found filled with the acrid smoke of gun powder.

The ghosts of Summerwind ended up being enough to cause the husband to have a complete mental breakdown and to cause the wife to attempt suicide. The family left Summerwind, and to their horror, found that Bober, the wife's father, had decided to buy the place and make a

11

restaurant out of it. Bober never actually lived in Summerwind, staying instead in a camper on the grounds. He reportedly had communicated with Carver and wrote his book to such an end.

The Bobers and their daughter's family were not the first, nor were they the last, in a long line of people whom Summerwind ejected, forcefully.

In the years since Bober's book was published, critics have poked many holes in the theories, but weird happenings have indisputably occurred. Many people have theories of their own regarding Summerwind, some make sense, and some, like the Carver theory, cause people to simply raise their eyebrows and say, "mmhmm."

Another theory has surfaced over time; this one, I think personally, has a stronger chance of being true. It is a theory brought to light by a woman out of Cleveland, Ohio, named Emily Forsythe Warren. She spent her childhood on West Bay Lake, the same lake that Summerwind inhabits. Her tale is one of treachery and sadness and rings true when forced through the sieve of history.

Miss Lucy of Lilac Hills

The story begins in the deep South following the Civil War. During the Reconstruction, transients, called carpetbaggers, moved throughout the South, looking for food, work, and shelter. They tended to move in groups, leaving destruction in their wake. In that era, despair pervaded the South, the wealth of the plantation families disappeared and these people, pampered and protected all their lives, found themselves facing ruin. It was not a pleasant prospect to people who prided themselves on the "blueness" of their blood. Blue-bloods formed the society of parties and socials, of wealth and accomplishment. Their society had been everything to them. They had slaves to take care of everything else.

Daughters of the plantations owners rarely found themselves taken seriously and usually were considered to be less valuable than the male slaves of the time. Some were kept almost as prisoners in the vast marble constructions with every comfort imaginable. Some were sent to powerful men's beds as concubines, and some were sold into marriage to men twice their age or complete strangers to seal a business deal.

Whitehall Plantation, just outside Atlanta, Georgia, found itself nearly destroyed by the carpetbaggers, and without the money and resources to rebuild. The Devereau family, owners of Whitehall, had three daughters. The plantation had many slaves and, before its downfall, had been one of the most productive and profitable in the area. Poverty was a great shock to the Devereau family. Life was hopeless for them, as none had any marketable skills and were not used to being part of the working class. In order to save her family, one of the three daughters, Lucy, who was the mistress of a very powerful New York banker by the name of Lamont, agreed to marry the son of the banker. Lamont bought the Whitehall Plantation and, because Lucy was marrying his son, allowed the family to continue living there.

Lucy agreed to marry Robert Patterson Lamont, son of her former lover, even though she did not love him, and moved to New York City to live with him. Her black servant from home, Hannah, moved with her. Lucy learned to become a part of New York society and very quickly took up the harp, as well as learning to speak several languages. She found enough to amuse herself and was relatively content in New York. However, Robert soon wanted to move.

Lamont built a magnificent mansion on the shores of West Bay Lake in Wisconsin in 1916. He called the place Lilac Hills and moved his wife, who was pregnant, and Hannah to it. He promised Lucy a great life in the "West."

Lilac Hills was appointed with many costly and beautiful items, Emily remembers velvet drapes and a silver candelabra, as well as "the biggest bellows I ever saw. It was some twelve feet across." There were spectacular stained glass windows and quarters for the servants.

At Lilac Hills, the Lamonts' first child, a boy named James, was born. Life seemed sweet for a few fleeting moments, but then Lamont's true nature revealed itself. Few other people lived in the area at the time and Lamont would not allow Lucy to leave Lilac Hills even to visit her family or friends.

Even though Lilac Hills was majestically appointed, Lucy hated it there from the very beginning; she was miserable. Lamont kept her a prisoner. Trappers, Native Americans, and the few neighbors tried to befriend Lucy, but Lamont chased them off. He kept her away from any outside contact.

Lucy was soon pregnant again, and she gave birth to a girl, whom they named Lucy. Baby Lucy died soon after she was born. She is buried on the property, and there is a small wooden marker in the trees that simply reads "Lucy."

The longer Lucy lived at Lilac Hills, the more miserable she became. Whenever she got the chance, she would post letters home to her family in Georgia, many telling strange tales of happenings at Lilac Hills. Tales of screams in the night and voices whispering imploringly "please come and see me" but, upon inspection, proved to have come from thin air, as there was no one present. Her son, James, began to act strangely, as well. The servants had unexplainable bruises all over their bodies.

The scariest place was the basement wine cellar. The entrance had been bricked over, but there were shackles imbedded in the walls themselves. It was a prison. Lilac Hills was a prison. Lucy had a strong urge to flee and get herself, Hannah, and her child out of harm's way.

Her husband hired an overseer to help control the lands, a man named John Whittington. Whittington befriended Lucy, and on one cold November day the four of them—Lucy, Whittington, James, and Hannah—fled over the railroad tracks to the near-by town of Ontonogon.

Robert instigated an exhaustive search, and the runaways were found in Virginia. Purportedly, Lucy was trying to get home to her family in Georgia. Patterson brought her back to Wisconsin, and nothing was heard about her for many years. Emily was under the impression that she was dead at the hands of her husband. However, she surfaced years later, a shell of the beautiful, witty woman she had once been. Her sad, terror-stricken life had taken its toll.

James was sent to boarding school in New York and proved to have become unbalanced enough from his time at Summerwind that he never entered the society he had been schooled to rule. Emily saw him years later, pumping gas at a small filling station in Wisconsin. She said his clothes were threadbare, but there was no doubt that it was James. She mentioned Lucy and Summerwind to him. His face slowly drained of color and took on a pinched quality. He warned her in a dreadful voice never, ever, to go to Summerwind again.

Emily spent her childhood with children of the few neighbors of the area. They roamed all over the woods and spent much time on the lake in a small boat. The children were given free reign over the area, but they were admonished never to go near Summerwind. However, when a storm came up suddenly, as happens in the Northwoods, the admonishments of their parents were cast aside for safety's sake and sent them scurrying for the shelter that Summerwind offered. They brought the boat to shore and scuttled under cover. As they entered the main door of Summerwind, they stopped, their breath caught in their throats. The place, which was abandoned then, looked as if it was lived in. Instead of the odors of mildew and decay, the delicate scents of lilac and old-fashioned lady's perfume pervaded the place, whiffs of tobacco smoke drifted on the puffs of air that circulated the room. There was a painting over the hearth of a beautiful woman. Her hair, the color of honey, hung past her shoulders, and her eyes were a clear blue, like that of West Bay Lake on a clear day. She was swathed in a white gown that looked to be pure gossamer silk. Her complexion radiated even through the imperfect medium of paint. The haunted expression behind her eyes echoed hollowly through those glowing orbs, however.

The children were standing in a perfectly appointed sitting room. The silk- and velvet-covered sofas and chairs were pulled cozily close to the massive fireplace. There were tables with delicately carved legs dotted around the room. Crystal vases glittered in the flashes of lightning through the silk-hung windows. Candlesticks and lamps shone from their places of state atop every flat surface in the room. There was no dust, no cobwebs, no air of disuse. The place looked ready for the great double doors to open and the servant to announce dinner.

One of the boys among the group of children kindled a fire in the massive fieldstone fireplace. Warmed and dried, the children decided to spend the rest of the storm exploring Summerwind. As a group, they tiptoed up the massive staircase. As they walked, gaping over the fine paintings and other furnishings, they heard footsteps behind them. They continued on a few steps further, but the clear sound of footsteps persisted. They turned. Standing on the third step was a woman. She was clothed in white. Her eyes were a beautiful blue, but they looked sad. She gazed upon them with those sad eyes, almost looking through the children standing before her, but then she smiled at them. Her face glowed as she smiled. She regarded them a second longer, then faded and was gone. There was no trace that she had been there, just a stronger scent of lilacs and lavender, and the

16

spot she had been standing seemed to catch a beam of light from somewhere. The children looked at one another in amazement, just as another bolt of lightning illuminated the room. The painting of the young woman looked at them from above the fireplace across the room. The expression on her painted face was much the same as the apparition that they had just seen. It was the same woman. It was Lucy. The only thing keeping the children from fleeing that very instant was the greater fear of electrocution from a lightning strike in the boat on the flat expanse of lake. That fear hit home when, a second later, the lake was hit with a bolt of lightning that followed with a crash of thunder loud enough to vibrate the breath from their chests for a few seconds.

Over the next few years, other storms sent the children to the dubious haven that Summerwind offered. They saw Lucy many more times. Each time, she was clothed in a white gown. One time, as they were running to escape the first few fat drops of an approaching storm, Lucy appeared on the porch, frantically waving her arms and motioning for them to get down. The children, who had no other option, dropped to the dampening ground. Suddenly shots rang out, and bullets zinged over their heads hitting trees and ricocheting off. The caretaker of the place was drunk and firing his rifle off the porch, shooting out into the storm. If Lucy had not warned them, the children could have been killed.

Another time, several years later, some men were moving a piece of heavy equipment across a small bridge near Summerwind, when a woman dressed in an old-fashioned white gown appeared on the bridge, motioning for them to stop. They did. Upon further investigation, the bridge was found to have become weak. It would never have held the weight of the men and the machinery. It would have buckled, and they would have crashed to their deaths. Lucy had saved another pair of lives.

Perhaps in vindication for being kept a prisoner in Summerwind, Lucy stays now to keep others from becoming tied to the place. In all accounts, Lucy is a sweet, sad-looking woman wearing a white dress.

Emily remembered those summer days with such clarity, I could almost feel my skin prickle when she told of Lucy first appearing to her and her friends on that stormy day.

The ghostly history that dogged Summerwind has roots to times long before any mention of Carver as the culprit. However, I needed to know more.

Armed with the life of Jonathan Carver, the life of Lucy Devereau-Patterson, and the immense history that pervades Summerwind, I knew that I had latched onto something. I had to see Summerwind for myself and perhaps visit the ghosts of Jonathan Carver and Miss Lucy.

I wanted to find it. I had to find it.

I had no notion of where to begin looking for Summerwind. The area purportedly bought in the deed is huge, and it would have taken a lifetime, if not several, to find the resting place of Carver's deed and Summerwind. Even though I told no one of this budding obsession of mine, somehow the information I needed to find seemed to find me. One cold, gray November evening, I received a call from an anonymous person who suggested that I try "north of Eagle River."

With that call, I knew it was north of my own place. I had narrowed my search area, and, elated with the new knowledge I possessed, I set out to find my prize.

The following day, I headed north on Highway 45 and drove every road I saw, and some tracks that were not even worthy of being called roads. I passed small town after small town, small cabin after small cabin, so many that they started to blur in my memory into one mass. I drove for hours, the November remnants of the deep woods seeping gloom into my bones as each turn seemed to yield nothing. As my LCD display clock on the dash flashed 4:00 P.M., with the woods getting darker by the second, a light snow started drifting down, sifting in between the branches of the huge trees that grew almost to the side of the road. Goaded by some invisible force, I flipped on my headlights and turned down one final road in one last desperate search for Summerwind.

It was a narrow road, probably impassable when winter's drifts locked it shut. Skeletal arms of the deciduous trees seemed to lock overhead while the spearhead shafts of the pines and spruce pierced the deep blue clouds covering the twilight sky. A few early stars poked through breaks in the clouds and twinkled what little I could see of the sky. My weary eyes scanned the land around the tree trunks and scrub brush on the side of the road. It was getting harder to see beyond the broad beams of my headlights, and I knew with a sinking-stomach dread that I would have to turn around and go home very soon. Just ahead, the road was a little wider, and I decided it was there that I would call it quits. I had given it my best shot, but I needed to get home before the snow locked me in and a snow plow, or spring, would have to rescue me. I braked slowly and carefully, as the snow had been making the roads slick, and just as I started the U-turn that would send me back to the warmth of my home and hearth, my headlights bounced off of something other than the damp trunks and raw cabins I had been seeing all day. Something large and black bulked through the trees. It had to be Summerwind.

I parked on the road, letting my headlights illuminate the house and began walking through the thick woods as the snow began to swirl harder. I could hear the snow landing on the smooth, open water of the lake beyond the house with a hissing sound, like a million whispers urging quiet. The trees overhead creaked as a gust of wind sent their tops a-swaying. My feet crunched through this fall's, as well as innumerable other falls', supply of dry leaves. I stepped over fallen branches and an entire tree that had laid itself out across the remnants of the driveway. The closer I got to the building, which was set back from the road quite a ways, the more convinced I became that I had found Summerwind.

The ground around the place was littered liberally with broken glass and beer bottles. Windows were gaping holes that looked like mortal wounds out of which the life of Summerwind had leaked. The clapboards of the siding were warped and twisted with neglect and the harsh winters of this northland. The whole house seemed to be sinking in on itself as it lost its battle against time and the elements. The only sounds that penetrated the deep silence of the place were the snow on the lake, the lapping of a few little waves and the moaning and groaning of the house itself as the wind played through it like a mighty pipe

Summerwind mansion was on its last legs when I took this photo in the spring of 1981.

organ. The hollow sounds that echoed through the clearing pulled my voice with them. I stood in the swirling snow, mute, with the cold seeping into my bones quickly. Emotions played over me—elation at finding Summerwind, no little fear of this haunted house and the eerie scene I had stumbled upon, and awe at the incredible dignity the place seemed to retain even though it had been dissected by revelers and the elements alike. The snow started falling faster, my headlights no longer able to illuminate the place. I stood in the cold for a few minutes more. Snow collected around my boots and settled, creating mini drifts. As the coating of snow grew thicker, it covered the ravages of time, and I could see a shadow of what the mansion must have looked like in its prime. I looked back to where my Bronco was waiting, the trail of my footprints, the only signs of life here, disappearing under the snow. I sighed, my breath hanging in white clouds in the air and turned to walk back to my truck. It was time to leave.

Several years passed before I went back to Summerwind. Finally, one fall day I ventured out to find it again. As I drove the dusky roads north, I could almost feel the cold seeping, once again, into my bones. After several wrong turns, I turned down a sandy side road. After driving forever down the bumpy road, I let my Bronco come to a rest on the soft side of the ditch, out of the right-of-way of any traffic, as unlikely as that was. I stepped from the warm cabin of the truck into the cold fall day. A huge wrought iron gate liberally hung with signs reading "no trespassing," "no hunting" and "private property" stood at the beginning of a driveway, a silent testament to the former opulence of the place. This was an entrance to Summerwind that I had not found on my previous trip to the mansion. I had, in essence, found Summerwind twice.

The gate was locked shut with several heavy chains and padlocks. Not wanting to force the issue, I stayed out-

21

side the gate and peered through the bars. Summerwind was barely visible from the heavy metal gate. What little I could see was not pretty. The Northwoods winters had not been kind to the mansion. It looked as if it were ready to fall down. The charred remains of many bonfires were stark monuments to the revelers that had imparted their effort in the demise of Summerwind. There were no windows remaining, and the shingles of the roof had been ripped off by wind and storm. The porch roof sagged deeply, matching the porch floor. Spray paint coated the remnants of walls with garish images. Bricks were crumbling and lay strewn about. A heavy wind or snow would probably be far too much for the weakening beams and nails to hold, and one of the greatest haunted houses would come crashing in on itself. However, a quiet end was not to be for Summerwind.

Fire Destroys Summerwind
Vilas County News-Review, June 22, 1988
A fire on Sunday, June 19, destroyed the Lamont mansion, one of Wisconsin's most notable haunted houses on West Bay Lake in Land O' Lakes. The fire at Summerwind is likely to have started by lightning, according to a fire department official.
Sam Otterpohl, Land O' Lakes fire chief and a neighbor, said there was a tremendous amount of lightning Sunday morning . . . However, Otterpohl said investigators were still not entirely sure of the cause.

All that remained were two chimneys and the cement stone patio. The fire destroyed the entire mansion as well as the servants' quarters and laundry building. A sorry end for a place that had been the pride and joy of the builders and filled with treasures collected over a lifetime. The remains were a monument to the frailty of the human existence.

Two massive fieldstone chimneys offer silent testimony to Summerwind's former grandeur on the shore of West Bay Lake.

After the fire, I thought that the legend of Summerwind would fade into vague memories, and the ghosts would find somewhere else to haunt. However, this was not to be.

23

I had talked about Summerwind briefly on a few radio shows where I was a guest during the Halloween season. After the fire, people began coming to me in droves to tell me their stories and experiences concerning Summerwind. Visits to Summerwind seem to be a trigger of sorts that manifested itself into pains, possessions, broken bones, depressions, and spooky stuff in general, and the people seemed to need to share their tales.

One of the first persons to talk to me about a strange incident—call it an exorcism—was a woman whom I'll call Cherie. She knew of the incident from first-hand knowledge. The other person to tell me about it was the local Northwood's pastor who performed the reported exorcism. The pastor sought me out to tell me the story. It was something he just had to get off his shoulders. I remember not saying a word as he told me the tale.

The young man had apparently become possessed after visiting Summerwind. His behavior could only be called strange at best. His friends sought the help of the local pastor when the young man reportedly started screaming in a voice not his own. His body contorted and the expression on his face was a ghastly twisted counterpane to the horrors he was cursing. Cherie said he screamed things so strange "you wouldn't believe it." He collapsed to the ground and shook with an internal struggle that was palpable to the onlookers. As foam started to form around his mouth, his eyes rolled up in his head, and he went limp. The pastor touched his forehead and drew back as if burned. He immediately started chanting a prayer, and the people gathered and formed a circle with hands clasped around the prone figure of the man. As each person picked up the prayer-chant, the body rose to a sitting position and started moving with jerks and twitches. A wind picked up and seemed to form a vortex above the body and swirled, alternately pulling and plastering the clothes of the people in the circle. Bits of debris from the ground — leaves and lit-ter — were pulled into the vortex and swirled around. A humming, like a thousand bees, built up underneath the sound of the chanting, until the vibrations alone were rum-bling in the chests of the participants, all other sound had gone silent. The jerking and twitching of the body in the circle became more and more intense until there was a "pop" that was more felt than heard. The man lay limp on the ground again. His face relaxed and his body calmed. The pastor dropped the hands of those next to him and knelt next to the man. He touched his forehead again and the worry on his face relaxed into a grim smile. The man's eyes flickered open, his eyes holding sense once again. He looked at the pastor with a mingling of fear and gratitude prevalent on his face. The pastor stood and extended his hand to the man and helped him up. His clothes had torn, "and the cross he wore around his neck burned into his chest," Cherie said. The man bears the scar from his encounter with the spirits of Summerwind to this day.

The stories did not stop there. People did not stay away. One evening the phone rang at the lodge. A male voice asked if I had a few moments to spare. Fearing a telemar-keter, I hesitated but agreed to listen.

"My name is Ray Rasmussen. I live near Rhinelander," he said. "I just had to call and tell you my stories." I could hear a TV somewhere in the background blaring country music. He paused for a moment before launching into the stories. I settled into a chair and prepared to take notes as he related to me his tales from Summerwind.

"It was in 1986, I believe," Ray told me, "when I visited Summerwind with some friends. And . . . the place had been trashed repeatedly. I did see the magnificent pool table in the basement. It, too, sadly, had been trashed. My friends and I were using a Ouija board . . . I'm into that stuff.

Summerwind as viewed through the camera lens of Bryan Adams.

"As the board started reacting to our questions, a wind suddenly blew wildly. As we were sitting on the floor in front of the fireplace, my friend [also] doing the Ouija stuff was suddenly hit in the head by a flying tile that had blown in through the window. My mouth dropped as it was a heavy tile and no ordinary wind could have ever moved it. I wanted no more to do with that kind of stuff."

Ray said he lurched to his feet and stumbled out of the rotting front doors, across the sagging porch and down the steps. Once he reached the bottom of the stairs he was stopped in his tracks as he noticed an unopened can of Miller beer sitting on the railing of the concrete stairs. It was fresh, the condensation on the side of the can gleaming wetly in the twilight. "It wasn't there when I entered. I was a teen then and would have noticed a beer. I hadn't, but it was there when I left." Ray grabbed the can and turned and sprinted to his car parked on the side of the road. He sat in his car and thought about what had happened to him and his friends. As for the beer, "I took it and I drank it." He remained in his car and waited for his friends to make their way out of the house. As the gloom gathered around him, he shivered. His friend had to go to the hospital to get stitches where the tile hit him in the head.

Ray and his friends were not scared enough and decided to return to Summerwind about a month after the tile incident. Again, he and his friends brought the Ouija board. They set up their board in front of the fireplace yet again. This time, taking the precaution of setting up candles and a lantern. It was lighter in the mansion this time, especially with the light cast by the candles. Ray was able to look over the walls. Apart from the depredations made by revelers and animals, the place looked eerily lived in, as if the house was waiting for the owners to get back from vacation. Furniture was all there, chairs and tables, books, lamps and dishes. Some were broken, most likely by the same revelers that had vandalized the walls, but most was intact and looked, though old, much loved and used. Ray and his friends settled in and began to use the Ouija board. Steeling themselves for another wind or some other method of revenge, they placed their hands on the glider. Nothing happened. A candle flame flickered in the simultaneous release of held breath. Suddenly, the glider seemed to jump to life and began spelling out words in rapid course. Words like "accident," "ambulance," "fire truck," "tow truck," and "cops." The boys looked at each other as the words poured from the board. The flickering candles cast creepy shadows over everything, and as the sun set outside, the shadows grew deeper and more sinister, each certainly containing something out of only the most fearful nightmares. Ray's friend Leslie chose that moment to come into the room from her explorations of the place, having not wanted to be a part of the Ouija board. Each of the men let out a yelp as she seemed to appear from the shadows, cobwebs hanging from her hair and clothes.

Their fears were getting the better of them, and they decided they had had enough of the weird words from the board. They grabbed their belongings and went outside to pile into Leslie's new Ford Escort.

In winter, the roads around Summerwind become very slick and treacherous. Due to the snow drifts from the wind and plows, the road narrows to make reaching the house extremely hazardous. As the road was fairly deep into the woods, it took several days before the plows could get to it, however, since the residents of the area were aware of this, they had chains to get themselves over the snow drifts until the plows came. Driving on the snow packed it into a solid sheet of ice. Coupled with the skim of frozen exhaust on top of that, the danger is immense, and extreme caution is always urged.

As Leslie was driving along, she noticed to her dismay that someone had parked his or her car in the middle of the road and was chasing a blowing object. The driver had thought it was a hat, however, the "hat" turned out to be a plastic bag blowing haphazardly in the strange wind patterns of Summerwind.

As Leslie approached, the brakes proved useless on the ice, and actually made them slide more, as she passed the car ever so gingerly. Just as she came level with the parked car, another car came head on just as the man stepped in front of his car. The next second seemed to take an eternity until the man landed with a sickening thud and crack on Leslie's windshield. The "accident" foretold by the Ouija board had struck the kids with a tremendous, life-changing force. The following events could have been funny, if the situation was not so deadly in earnest. The ambulance arrived but quickly slid into the deep snow on the side of the road and, without chains, became stuck. A fire truck came. It too soon mired in the road. The tow truck came, as did the cops—all foretold in the strange, eerie meeting inside Summerwind.

The man who was struck died three days later.

Amazingly, Ray returned with friends to Summerwind on November 13, 1994.

"My sister took a picture with her Polaroid," Ray said. "And there on the concrete railing where I had spotted and taken the Miller beer can was a small white mist. It was right there in the exact same spot."

I could hear the chill creeping into his voice, even over the phone. The rest of the pictures seemed to be okay, except almost all of them had strange shadows that could not have come from the flash. It was almost as if someone kept following them with a lantern, keeping just out of sight . . .

A DIALOGUE WITH JONATHAN CARVER

On a muggy Friday, June 17, 1994, the phone rang. It was a woman named Lynn Renor of Madison, Wisconsin. She had sent me a letter detailing some of the exploits of Jonathan Carver and the search for his deed. She wondered if she and some friends could stop by to relate some details of an encounter they had had. She came over with friends

Lynn Renor reports on the Ouija board responses with the spirit of Jonathan Carver while Tariq Eyssa watches.

Julie Wood, Ramy Renor, and Julia McPeek. Later, Lynn's boyfriend Tariq Eyssa would join us on the front porch overlooking Trout Lake.

Their story, told in an excited and enthusiastic manner, began with the Ouija board. The board, they said, spelled out "Summerwind on the shore of West Bay in Land O' Lakes," which was, by then, a pile of rubble. The board also revealed several more clues: a half-circle shape and "30 feet."

Lynn, who penciled out feelings from the Ouija board experience, revealed several characteristics of an alleged communication.

— weaving around letters before selecting one
— sharp, abrupt stops
— very strong, quick movements
— shortcuts
— If the group guessed what the spirit was saying, the spirit would go directly to yes or no and not finish the thought.
— few mistakes, easy to understand
— when waiting for a question, the spirit would hover the pointer under the word Ouija

The girls were compelled to visit Summerwind, and they did so at midnight on June 16. They drove down the long country roads. As they drove, the moon, which was in the half-moon stage, appeared with fast-scudding clouds blocking the light from time to time. Watching the moon appear and disappear, suddenly they realized that the half circle on the Ouija board was a so-called "half-moon."

Driving down the sandy gravel road that is the only access to Summerwind, they were impressed by the darkness beneath the trees, places that the intermittent moonlight did nothing to illuminate. The girls watched for the haunted house carefully, hoping not to miss it as they drove slowly down the road. Suddenly the gleam of the gate caught the eye of one girl, and she let out a little shriek, it became obvious to each of them just how tense the situation was becoming. The girl driving directed the car to the soft shoulder of the road and shut off the engine. Other than the ticking of cooling metal, no sounds penetrated the thick and heavy darkness and gloom. Flitting forms moved about, visible only when the moon appeared from behind the clouds. The girls realized that these were probably bats, making a feast off the bugs that live near the lake and surrounding area. Putting on a bravado that they did not feel and grabbing shovels from the trunk of the car, the girls crossed the road to stand beneath the heavy iron arches of the gate. It was like something out of a horror movie, with the iron gleaming in such a way that it appeared to glow whenever the moon put in an appearance. The gate was locked and chained, but the fence that surrounded the property was simple barbed wire and easily crossed. One girl held the wire apart as the other girls wriggled through. Once all were on the other side, every hair on their arms stood on end and an errant breeze stirred

Sharing their experiences of the midnight visit to Summerwind mansion are, from left, Julia McPeak, Lynn Renor, Julie Wood, and Ramy Renor. They trekked north from the Madison area.

the hair on their necks. Biting their lips, one by one they stepped forward and cautiously walked onto the ancient driveway. The girl who had taken the lead stepped on a stick that broke beneath her weight with a crack. The other girls stopped short, but not for long. Overhead, an owl, disturbed by their presence, made itself known with a hoot that echoed in the thick silence. The start from the owl, once they realized what it was, got them moving again with wry and wary smiles on their lips. A few more steps further, and they were suddenly engulfed in a gigantic cloud of mosquitoes that bit them from every angle. Despite every attempt to shield themselves from the attack, it persisted. Almost as one, they turned and fled back to the safety of their car. As soon as they changed their direction and intention, however, the attack stopped and the were able to return to the car unmolested by any other wildlife.

They asked the spirit or whatever if they should leave—was evil lurking? The message received, Lynn said, was that all should leave. The spirit identified itself as Jonathan Carver and claimed to be searching for his deed. The conversation with Jonathan Carver's spirit was enlightening in some respects, as he hinted at a gate or passage that was bringing bad spirits to haunt Summerwind. He suggested that the bad spirits were drawn to the place and that it was not safe for human beings to inhabit the place any longer. He also said that the number of spirits had increased greatly in the previous several months.

After leaving their shovels behind them as ordered by the spirit, who said they were in a risky situation, they drove into the dark. There above them, the moon turned red. A red moon of blood, they felt. They drove off, the roads themselves seemed to be twisting and turning in ways that the girls had not remembered. They got lost. They drove down the dark roads, heading away from Summerwind, taking any turn that seemed even remotely

Julie McPeak talks about the group's night of terror and the strange happenings at Summerwind.

familiar. After driving for about a half an hour, the girls knew that they were not going in the right direction. One dirt road after another looked the same; there were no signs or distinguishing features. The girls stared at the reflections of their faces white and drawn from fear in the glass of the

33

car windows. They drove in silence, hoping that somehow the next turn would look familiar.

Julie Wood was in the back seat to the right of Ramy. "Suddenly, I had this feeling of power . . . perhaps there was a bad spirit in the car. I felt almost numb, and there was a tingling in my arm. I felt larger than life, almost like I wasn't there. It was tense in the car. My heart was pounding savagely. I had an enormous feeling of strength. I was lightheaded. That moment—I was tall, powerful and tingling. I felt so powerful, I could move the moon. It was now very bright. It was a red moon."

She told the others in a voice that was hushed and subdued of her feelings, and at once the driver pulled off the road, coming to a stop on the soft needle-covered shoulder. The girls immediately piled out of the car and formed a tight circle around Julie. They chanted and prayed, and as quickly as it had come, the feeling of power left Julie. She sank to the ground with weariness and sobbed with relief.

Summerwind at Night

I first ran across the photo of Summerwind at night through a photographer named Dannie. She, too, was haunted by the immense presence of the Summerwind mansion near Land O' Lakes, Wisconsin.

The picture is haunting. Taken on the night of the full moon, Dannie revealed that there was a series of strange happenings in the photo. It was taken at midnight through 12:05 A.M.

"There were five things that are unusual about the photo," Dannie claimed. "There are things there that couldn't be explained twelve hours later." Dannie said the photo revealed two silhouettes, a "gargolish" face at top left, a ghostly skull on smaller roof at right, and adds that the lights appear to be on "even though I used a flash."

As the full moon was rising over the Northern Highland State Forest, a great blue heron swept into view. Imagine the wail of a common loon in the background, a warm campfire, and some eerie ghost stories in a nearby campground and you have a dose of summer magic in the Northwoods.

Dannie added: "The reflections of the flash and the feeling that the lights were on didn't match the angle of the walls."

Her photo is eerie at best, wish I had it now.

35

PART TWO

OTHER TALES

THE PAULDING LIGHTS

The Mysterious Lights of Watersmeet
Vacationers and locals alike visit the mysterious lights some five miles north of Watersmeet, Michigan, just west of Highway 45 on the Robbins Pond Road.

According to one legend, the first sighting was in 1966 when a carload of fun-seekers stopped near a swampy area, called Dog Meadow, on an old military road. They sat in their car, laughing and talking, when the temperature seemed to rise suddenly. The chatter was bitten off suddenly as a brilliant light filled the inside of the car. Each person drew in a sharp breath when after a sudden flash, the light glowed far too bright to look at. The teens looked out the windows of the car and saw that the strange lights were making the power lines paralleling the road glow with a brilliance, too. For several minutes, the lines glowed in all directions as far as the kids could see, outlining roads for several hundred yards at least. The glow began to fade, slowly, and soon there was nothing left but the normal bare wires and the soft glow of indicator lights on the dash

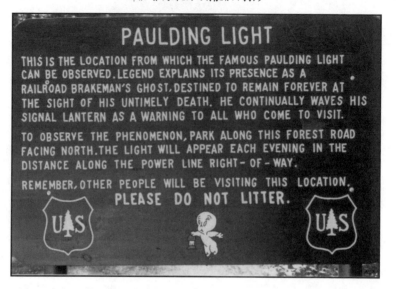

PAULDING LIGHT

THIS IS THE LOCATION FROM WHICH THE FAMOUS PAULDING LIGHT CAN BE OBSERVED. LEGEND EXPLAINS ITS PRESENCE AS A RAILROAD BRAKEMAN'S GHOST, DESTINED TO REMAIN FOREVER AT THE SIGHT OF HIS UNTIMELY DEATH. HE CONTINUALLY WAVES HIS SIGNAL LANTERN AS A WARNING TO ALL WHO COME TO VISIT.

TO OBSERVE THE PHENOMENON, PARK ALONG THIS FOREST ROAD FACING NORTH. THE LIGHT WILL APPEAR EACH EVENING IN THE DISTANCE ALONG THE POWER LINE RIGHT-OF-WAY.

REMEMBER, OTHER PEOPLE WILL BE VISITING THIS LOCATION.
PLEASE DO NOT LITTER.

The sign posted by the U.S. Forest Service features a Casper-like character with a lantern. (Photo courtesy Virgil Beck.)

panel. The kids looked around at each other, the whites of their eyes large in the dim light.

Old timers near Watersmeet, and Paulding, Michigan, to the north, claim that the legend started many years before when a railroad switchman was crushed to death between two railroad cars while attempting to signal the train's engineer. He had been carrying a lantern and moving along the track. He was trying to signal an "All aboard," when the train lurched into motion, just as his foot slipped and he fell between two cars that jolted and bumped into one another, crushing him. His lantern crashed to the ground, smashing the glass and spreading burning kerosene in a flaming pool around him. His horrid screams were heard, until the flames from the kerosene licked up the side of the cars and his face and voice were gone. Men on the platform rushed to get gunny sacks and water to attempt to put out the fire, but it was far too late by the time the vicious flames subsided. The pitiful, broken remains of the switchman were pulled from between the cars, and people remarked that the horror was so prominent on his face that it hurt to look at him. He was buried in the small graveyard near there, but perhaps his ghost is condemned to atone for his mistake and stupidity by guarding the tracks near there and flashing his warning lights to any trains that pass.

Another tale that has persisted in the area is that the lights are the ghostly beams of the flashlight of a mail carrier that was murdered, along with two of his dogs, in Dog Meadow over a hundred years ago. Mail was carried on horseback then, and it was customary that it would be one man's job to ride relay from town to town making sure the mail got through, no matter the weather or the obstacles.

The man had been riding his horse through the swampy meadow. It was late fall, and he had to be very careful, watching for skim ice that could signify deep water.

He rode the route every day, going back and forth between Paulding and Watersmeet. He always kept his faithful hounds by his side when he made that trek, some ten miles of wilderness with few houses. He knew the area down to the last hand's-breadth.

He noted with relief that the slight rise signifying the end of the marsh ground was only a few horse-lengths away. The muscles in his neck relaxed slightly, calming after the treacherous passage of the swamp. He could feel the horse's relief as well.

Just as he was just about to come out of the swampy area, the report of a rifle reached his ears. He flattened himself in his saddle instinctively. He called his dogs with a harsh whisper. Too late, with a yelp, one dog was down, shot through the neck. Another report, and the other dog fell. The man craned his neck in the direction of the rifle shots, but saw no one. He quickly dismounted from his horse and lay flat on the ground, the wet, cold, mucky soil wetting his clothing.

For several minutes, all was silent. No sounds except the beating of his own heart and the movements of the horse reached his ears. The lifeless forms of his two dogs lay on the soggy ground with their blood mingling with mucky water. Cold leached into his body, a numbness that followed fast on the heels of the racking cold. A tear for his faithful friends escaped his eyes, but the bitter wind quickly ripped even that small amount of comfort away. He lay in the silence so thick it weighed down upon him. Silence, bleak and black. Suddenly, not too far away, a stick cracked. The sound ricocheted in his head. Too close, far too close. Silence oozed around him again, like the soft mud into which his knee was sinking. No more sounds reached his ears until the quiet metal click of a hammer being drawn back on a rifle. Another noise followed, one that seemed too loud and too quiet at the same time. Sluggish thoughts surfaced in his mind. It felt as if his life was draining away somehow. It occurred to him that he should be feeling pain, but there was no pain. Harsh laughter bubbled into the sticky blackness in which he found himself floating. Laughter and then a new kind of silence — peaceful and light.

His body was found by a search party several days later. His dogs lay beside their master in death as they had walked beside him in life. His horse was never found. Searchers followed the footprints in the mud for half a mile or so, but then they too disappeared. The mail he was carrying was strewn over the meadow and most was never found.

The lights are thought to be his soul, searching for the man who killed him and his two dogs. Evermore on a quest to make sure the mail got through.

Yet another legend concerns a tavern owner. Long ago when the railroad still ran through the area, a station or town was sometimes only marked by a crudely painted sign and perhaps an inn or tavern.

Such a place stood in the midst of the wilderness near a swampy meadow in the Upper Peninsula of Michigan. It was a combination inn and tavern, offering shelter to the few travelers on foot and the railroad passengers who disembarked there, as well as a gathering place for the sporadic settlers of the area. The owner was a jolly man who looked after the inn and catered to the needs of the weary traveler with a delight that few people have had the privilege of experiencing. He acted as mayor for the scattered houses that formed a loosely organized village.

Together with his wife, he tended to the needs of any who found themselves under his jurisdiction. One of the many duties he took upon himself was to check the tracks for as far as he could see and then meet the night train with a lantern, letting them know all was well and the track was clear. He did this for years. The engineer relied on him, because in such a wild area it was not unheard of for a deer or moose to die on the tracks, or for a tree to fall over and land on the tracks. Such dangers would spell doom for the train and its precious cargo of settlers.

Time passed, and he was well known and loved because of his constant devotion to the comforts of his guests and the townsfolk. His civic involvement and love consumed much of his time, and the remaining was spent presiding over the beer barrels in his tavern. However, this left little time to devote to familial matters. After several years of patience and a deficit of attention, his wife became entangled with a passing peddler who roomed at the inn for several days. When the peddler moved on into the new territory hawking his wares to those who rarely saw anything but homespun, much less the bright-colored ribbons he carried in his pack, the innkeeper's wife left with him. The pair sneaked out in the dead of night, slipping away without notice.

The next morning, the inn keeper looked about for his wife, but found no sign of her. Noting the peddler also gone, he asked questions. One of the trappers whose lines ranged far south of town had said that he had seen a lantern light dancing in the trees and heard voices, a man's and a woman's, while he was working his lines very early in the morning.

Logic concluded that his wife had left with the peddler. The innkeeper was devastated. For the first time since its inception, the inn did not open its massive doors with the dawn. The innkeeper kept a solitary watch over the steadily lightening sky. His bleary eyes watched the glowing orb of the sun begin its daily trek across the rose-tinged bowl of the heavens. All day, the man sat perched upon a stool gulping down the strong beer the inn kept in stock.

The time came when he would have donned his scarf and grabbed his lantern to go and check the track, he was in no condition to walk. He lay slumped over the bar, no longer conscious of anything but the aching of his broken heart. Time passed with little recognition. He did not notice when a storm blew up in the northwestern sky and raced toward the little settlement. He did not notice when the wind picked up, tossing leaves and sending trees aswaying. He did not notice the shutters beating themselves into splinters against the weathered clapboard siding of the inn. Nor did he notice the far-off pinprick of light that moved through the trees. The train was coming. His lantern sat on the little shelf by the door. The chimney had been cleaned the night before, the reservoir filled with kerosene. His scarf hung on the hook below the shelf. He lay in a pool of spilled liquor, no longer feeling anything.

The engineer was thrown off. His sense of time and direction, already skewed in the storm, was obliterated without the cheerful beam from the lantern to flash him the "all's well." As he passed the darkened bulk of the inn, he wondered about the fate of the faithful innkeeper.

Rain sheeted past the windows of the train. The lights reflected on the drops; thousands of tiny mirrors danced on the winds that whipped them about. The track shone wetly, and the gravel and ties gleamed in the lamp light. Trees swayed in the wind as they flashed past, each catching in the light for a second before the train had moved on. The lamp light made a rough circle that displayed the wilderness around the track only seconds before the train passed. There was never enough time to register any landmarks, and on a night like that, with no moonlight to aid the visibility and the rain and wind adding to the confusion, no one could see anything.

Suddenly something flashed into view. The intervening seconds between the time the engineer noticed the tree trunk laying across the track like a sleeping serpent and the train slammed into it seemed to take forever—and yet no time at all. The train derailed, the engine crashed itself into the woods near the track. The impact caused the boiler to explode. Fire rained down on the sodden landscape.

Everyone on board the train that night perished.

When dawn approached, light crawled over the mangled iron and broken bodies strewn around the site like so many wind-blown leaves. The village was alerted, and soon people were crawling over the wreckage pulling the bodies out. The innkeeper was not one of the ones who went out to the scene. He could not bear to see what his carelessness had done.

Found amongst the burned, scalded and mangled bodies, were two who had not been on the train. The innkeeper's wife and the peddler had been following the track. They had camped near the track, so as not to get lost in the tractless wilderness. They had not traveled far from the village before they camped.

The innkeeper sat in the dark of his inn and waited for the rebuff from the townspeople to reach him. When it never came, he ventured out only to be greeted by looks of sorrow and pity. The man who had stood so high over the people giving every vestige of his strength to see to their comfort was now a fragile shell of a man, broken. He had failed in his two most important duties. His wife was gone, and the faith of the town was wavering. He died soon after. One fateful night had snuffed out over one hundred lives.

It is said that the lights seen are those of his wife and the peddler making their escape and that of the innkeeper himself flagging down the train, condemned to forever do what he had failed to do in life. The warning stands as a vigil to anyone who becomes too consumed in work.

Still others say the light is the ghost of the wrecked train, forever doomed to make its ill-fated run until the end of time.

Getting to Robbins Pond Road is easy, just off Highway 45 between Paulding and Watersmeet, Michigan. Although mainly visible at night, the lights can frequently be seen during the day.

The lights are seen on most clear nights any time of the year. Some motorists seeing the lights think they are the headlights of an on-coming car and swerve to avoid it.

One investigator, a security chief at a major Milwaukee-area department store, said she saw two lights—one small, one large. "Those lights moved close together, then apart," she said. "Sometimes the lights would change color from white to red, and then to dim green."

Most light lookers claim the strange glows are the headlights of cars, traffic in the distance along Highway 45. The road bends several times, making that possible. Others say the lights are reflections from nearby quartz rocks refracting headlights.

One Rhinelander resident said, "It can't be all headlights. Heck, the Indians reported seeing lights there before cars were even in use."

Another Theory on the Lights

A man named Pete said the lights resembled the intense beams seen on Mississippi River barges. Those beams are very intense but only if looking at them directly. The Watersmeet lights have a direct intensity, and then seem to fade and come back again at full strength. Pete said something like that might be the key to the entire mystery of the lights.

"It's probably a lighthouse on Lake Superior," he said.

Those watching for the lights in Dog Meadow are looking north toward Lake Superior. There are many lighthouses there and that could trigger the strange lights. A line drawn from the Robbins Pond Road-Dog Meadow area directly north comes close to Ontonogon, Michigan, with Lake Superior stretching out beyond that.

The point of the light sightings is a continental divide. All water north of that point flows north toward Superior and Hudson Bay. South of it, water eventually finds the Mississippi River and the Gulf of Mexico. In other words,

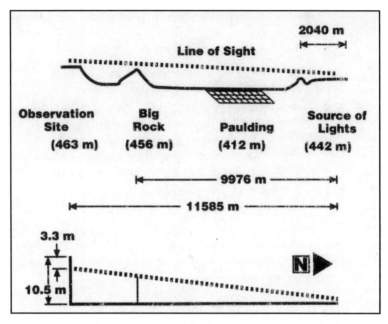

Elevation is another key to the mystery lights. A few meters to the north and the lights are no longer visible. It is thought that the streetlights in Paulding contribute to the effect. (Photo courtesy *Wisconsin Academy Review*.)

Dog Meadow area is a peak, some 1,700 feet above sea level. Light watchers are seated on a high place while looking north toward Lake Superior. This gives credence to Pete's lighthouse theory.

Virgil Beck's Experience at Watersmeet

Naturalist and wildlife artist, Virgil Beck of Stevens Point told of his experience shared with friends about 11:00 P.M. on Sunday, August 14, 1994, when the moon was at first quarter.

"I saw the light," he said, "and I kept telling myself it was the moon. My friends said, 'No,' it was the ghost light. It was darker than a street light—yellowish orange. It was irregular in shape, like a chunk of a jigsaw puzzle. The light

This map is a key to solving the light mystery. Those observing the lights believe that they are looking west, as I did the first time. However, the Robbins Pond Road, after a quick jog, aims north and zeros in on Highway 45 in the Jackson and Erickson Lakes region. The observation site is also a key, the top of Big Rock. It is probable that the lights are vehicle lights seen at a distance of six miles. (Map courtesy of the *Wisconsin Academy Review*)

moved in and out of the trees. Through the leaves, I kept telling myself it was the moon.

"The light was strange—orangish, yet yellowish. I told my friends that the coloration was due to the level it was at the horizon, an atmospheric effect."

Beck then told of a happening with one of the women who had come along. "As we were walking along the road, looking for the lights, suddenly this woman became frightened, almost frantic. Two of the guys grabbed her wrists to try to calm her down, she seemed so terrified. She said she could sense something was near. Soon after that we saw the light, which I labeled the moon. Later I checked, and it couldn't have been the moon.

"I saw the light settle down behind the brush. The moon doesn't do that. The moon is more constant, yet the light was dipping through the leaves. The moon doesn't get brighter or darker as the Watersmeet light does.

"It really resembled a jigsaw blob. The color struck me as that of the hand in those don't-walk signs on street corners—orangish. Then I thought the color reminded me of the lava seen when a volcano erupts at night—those globs or blobs.

"Leaves were covering part of the light. I couldn't get a clear idea of its shape. That was weird. Then I thought it was intelligent, trying to hide from us behind the leaves. Perhaps it was trying to camouflage itself. That's the sense I had. Then I perceived the light was red or white.

"I'll never forget the way that woman friend had a conniption fit . . . back in the car, she was shaking . . . tremors, if you will, and very cold."

A Letter from Marlene Voll

Marlene Voll of West Bend, Wisconsin, was fascinated by the mystery lights of Watersmeet and shared an experience she and some family members had.

"My mom, two daughters and a son all went to the area of the lights one day in October 1992. My parents have a cabin in the woods. They have no phone, no electricity, no city water, only bottled gas, a wood stove and an oil stove, and an outhouse."

Four and one-half miles north of Watersmeet, Michigan, Robbins Pond Road lures tourists from all over the world to observe the strange phenomenon known as the Paulding lights. The lights occur during early darkness, during all seasons, and in all kinds of weather.

The family gathered around the glowing stove in the cabin. It was decided that the next day Marlene's husband would be spending time doing one of his favorite activities: bow hunting. Her father would be cutting wood. Marlene, her mother, and her children decided that they would drive

49

the few miles to the Dog Meadow area and see if they could see the famed lights

"We saw it as we were driving. We asked some guys if it was the mystery light, and they said it was. We were so overwhelmed and excited. We saw the green light, a red one, and, of course, the white light. At one time it stayed for seven minutes. We watched it for a long time.

"I took a picture of it, too. Big, big mistake! Do not take a picture of the light. Going back towards my parents' cabin on Highway 55, we ran into major trouble. Our Cherokee Jeep decided to die in Conover near a bar called the Log Cabin. Fortunately the people there were very nice.

"The Jeep died about a quarter block south of the bar. It just slowed down and came to a complete stop. I was so scared. The Jeep wouldn't start up again, and, in fact, it didn't make a sound! That was about 7:30 P.M. Saturday.

"We had some guys look at it. I called Crandon police to see if they'd drive to the cabin to have my dad and husband come help us. No luck. We waited, hoping they were on their way, but nope. I called again. Finally, at 11:45 P.M. I called a towing service in Crandon. I told the man my dad and husband were at the cabin and to please drive past that way and tell them.

"At midnight, I called the towing service back to see if he had left, and his wife said he had. At 1:00 A.M., the police finally got to the cabin and the tow truck was five minutes after them. At 2:25 A.M., my husband and dad finally arrived. This was after seven hours in a bar with three small kids.

"Anyway, it cost sixty dollars to tow the Jeep plus a new fuel pump. The strange thing was that the mechanic said fuel pumps just don't die like that."

Marlene added, "A friend at work said she used to live in Eagle River, and she's seen the light, too. She also said her aunt will never go back to the light. She took a whole roll of film. None of the pictures turned out, and her car died between the military road and the one the light is on in Watersmeet."

The Watersmeet Lights by Motorcycle

Jim, a gas station attendant, related this tale: "I went up there on my 1987 Harley motorcycle, and something strange happened. I saw the light and started to ride at it. Suddenly, my cycle started to sputter, as if it was out of gas. I thought perhaps the gas line had been nicked off, so I looked down. It was on. Yet the engine died. As I walked away from the light, pushing the Harley, it started in a snap. Pretty strange."

Seeing the Light

Three days before Christmas 1994, Ron Eckstein sent me a report, "The Mystery of the Paulding Lights," by James Seal, Lisa Lombardi-Rice, and William P. Rice. On top of the first page, Ron had penned, "Mystery solved."

The lights between Paulding and Watersmeet, Michigan, are seen from a hilltop four and one-half miles north of Watersmeet along Old Military Road, also known as Robbins Pond Road.

The three who contributed to the scholarly piece cited a brochure they had been given that listed a number of common explanations for the lights: the spirit of the dead mail carrier, the ghost of the railroad engineer killed in a railroad accident and/or a mystical religious manifestation.

The trio of ghost-light busters asked open-ended questions of the locals and other interested spectators, questions like, "What color was the light?" rather than "Was the light red?" This tended to obtain details from the observers. For the most part the group questioned agreed on their descriptions. After an intense and thorough investigation, the trio reached this conclusion:

We have identified the source of the Paulding Lights. They result from vehicle lights seen at a distance of six miles, originating from a section of Highway 45 near Johnson and Erickson Lakes. Street lights in the town of Paulding, enhanced by atmospheric conditions such as mist, contribute to the effect.

Just When You Thought It Was Safe to Go Back to Watersmeet

The light mystery might be solved by what Ron sent me, but, on Saturday night, March 11, 1995, the "scientific" theory went the way of the wild goose.

Anne Keegan, of the *Chicago Tribune*, came for a visit with husband Len Aronson. She was up doing a story on public radio station WXPR. Nick VanderPuy, one of the story finders of the station, took Anne to show her the mystery lights.

Anne talked about her experience, saying that she did not see the light. Apparently, the light is a sometimes thing. Then she said something totally out of the blue. "I may not have seen the light, but something strange did happen. My phone wouldn't work, and the radio went dead. It sure was strange. The only thing making it through on the radio was a religious station."

That certainly wasn't car lights.

THE TALE OF TOBIE

In the early days of World War II, spirits ran high, and people responded by volunteering for any job that came along. My father took off with the Army Corp of Engineers to help build a highway to Alaska. Dad, whose trade as a printer was not as exciting as this new adventure, was too old to join the military service. Three older brothers each chose different branches of the service during the war, so Mom was left at home with my younger sister and me. It wasn't an easy time for us, just coming out of the Great Depression. The monthly government checks helped a lot.

We had a small house. Mother and my sister shared a bedroom on the ground floor, and I had to sleep in the attic. It was small, but it was our home and it was cozy.

An old coal-fired furnace chugged away daily, but at night Mom turned it down to its lowest setting to save the coal, and we burned anything else lying around.

My bedroom was accessed through steep steps that had a trap door in the attic floor, usually kept closed. Naturally, to conserve heat, the door also remained closed in the winter. My breath seemed to hang like a cloud when it was twenty degrees below zero outside, and I tried to conserve precious body heat under a fluffy down quilt Mom made for me. Rusty, a little mutt that strayed into our yard one day became my companion and alternate heater. Mom did not like Rusty in bed with me—doggie prints on the clean sheets, I guess—but she never stayed around in that frigid room long to check on the dog and me. Come washday, she knew just where the dog slept at night and gave me that pinched look to let me know that this practice was not to be tolerated. However, faced with the choice between freezing and making mother angry, I chose to make my mother angry. Rusty stayed.

Most of my childhood friends were threatened by the idea that the "bogeyman" would get them if they didn't behave. I believed it as a pure fact of life, no question in my mind. Each night before going to bed, I searched my closet and under my bed with meticulous care, searching for any sign or shadow that could be the bogeyman lurking. I always made sure that the adjoining attic room was closed off with a chair propped under the door handle. I even sat on the chair to make sure it was jammed in there good and hard. Beyond that door lay the deeper, darker part of the attic where something lurked that I just did not care to meet. I had ventured in there one day, in broad daylight; the light never seemed to reach very far into the place. It was as if the darkness swallowed it and spit out the shadows and creepy noises. My mother told me with an exasperated voice that it was just shadows and my own folly. However, after that day, I was even more sure that it was not me, that the bogeyman had to be real.

The bogeyman was real. On one of those cold, cold nights when more than one little dog under the covers would have been ideal, something woke me, and the dog started shivering in spasms. Knowing he wasn't cold, I put my head under the covers. I didn't want to look. I heard a kind of breathing sound; it came from near me and to the left, as if someone was standing over me from the side of the bed. I tried to tell myself that it was just my imagination. But the dog knew it was there, and so did I. I finally drifted off to sleep after at least an hour of lying there rigid with fear. When I woke in the morning, I pulled the covers from my face very slowly, hoping that whatever had been breathing was gone. There was no one in my room, but when I looked toward the dark side of the attic, I saw that the door to the back attic was wide open after I had carefully propped the door shut as usual. I dove back under the covers, not wanting to put my feet down on the cold floor. The door being open proved to me that something had been there in the night. It came many times after that and would stand next to or hover over my bed.

I eventually learned that there was no reason to fear this thing. I never told Mom about it or anyone else until recently. I firmly believe this spirit adopted me and followed me through the rest of my life. Too many things have happened to me to disregard its power and influence.

Time has erased details of these childhood encounters, but the memories were brought back with a clarity that was almost frightening with a new encounter. It began a couple of months after I had moved into a small apartment in a building I own, built in the 1920s. A business is located in the front of the building, and the basement runs the full length of the building but is not used much other than for storage. The small apartment consists of one bedroom, a kitchen-living area, and a bath. A hallway runs from the business front past the bedroom and bath to the rest of the unit.

Early one Sunday morning when lying half awake, I head the name "Tobie" called out in a long, moaning voice that sounded like "Tooowwwbeee." I thought at first it was someone playing a joke on me. My building is located next to a bar, but after looking at the clock, I saw it was after 2:00 A.M., and the place was closed. By then I was lying in bed, very wide awake, when I felt the edge of the bed settle down, as if someone or something sat down next to me.

At that time, I had a cheap telephone. It sat on the floor and had no cradle. To achieve a dial tone, all I had to do was pick it up or move it. Something did move it, and I heard the 'ding' of the dial tone. A dim light came in from the window, but I couldn't see anything and wasn't making a strong effort to do so. Only a moment after the phone noise, I felt as if I was covered with the lightest down cover—almost like the static of a balloon near my skin. Then an electrical field moved up and down my body. It wasn't frightening, and I thought at first it was chilblains or hairs rising on my skin. Later, this electrical charge was repeated so many more times that I was convinced it was not just my nerves going wacky.

At times a week or more passed before I would experience the presence of what I called, "Tobie." Every time, Tobie would ding the phone—until I finally removed it—to let me know it was there. After the phone was gone, it found other ways of getting my attention before I got the electric charge. A rap on the wall, hitting a cardboard box or rapping the phone cord on the dresser was enough. The electrical charge was always the same and lasted no more than six or eight seconds. One night I was visited three times between two and five A.M. The visitations were almost always early in the morning, and Tobie always made sure I was clearly awake.

On one occasion, while doing some entry work on my computer, a calculator on another desk started operating itself. I told myself that Tobie had just learned something new. I walked over to the desk and turned the machine off and got the electrical charge standing up in the middle of the day. I sat down at the desk with the calculator just to think about this new mystery when the calculator started running again.

Recently, a lady friend stayed with me, and we had a very amazing experience. About 3:00 A.M., right above our heads came a loud "ping" noise, a sound close to what that old phone made but completely artificial. I asked my lady friend if she had heard it, not knowing if she was sleeping at the time. She said she had. Just about that time, I felt the electrical charge and told her that Tobie was with me. She hollered, "Get away!" and jumped up from the bed. She ran into the bathroom and would not come back, even after Tobie left.

We talked about the experience several times afterwards, and we agreed that the ping was unlike any sound produced by an instrument or mechanical means.

One thing that bothered me was that different employees have worked in the front business office, and none of them have ever been bothered by strange events, other than the fire alarm would start buzzing occasionally even though it had new batteries. The alarm would buzz, yet no one smoked and no cooking was being done at the time.

Author's note: The teller of this tale lived in Minocqua, Wisconsin. He has since moved away to the north shore of Lake Superior.

THE MYSTERY OF TROUT LAKE

Muffy's parents loved their home on south Trout Lake. They created the place to be a retirement home and haven for themselves and their daughter Muffy. Meticulous care had gone into the construction and furnishing of the place.

Muffy's father had had a painting done of himself by a friend who was a painter. He hung the painting above the hearth in the greatroom of the place. He was very fond of the painting, and so was Muffy's mother.

Sadly, before they could make a good life in the place, both parents were tragically killed in a boating accident. But, after their deaths, a most strange and bizarre series of incidents occurred as related by Muffy St. Germaine.

Muffy told the following story:

"We heard something [one] night," she said. "It was downstairs, so we went to see what the sound was. There on the floor, far from where it had been on the wall, lay the oval-framed painting of my father [Bob Schiller]. Someone or something had moved it . . . or it moved by itself.

"It couldn't just have fallen off the wall, especially where it ended up on the floor. It would have to have rolled one way, then another, and then made another right turn to get where we found it. I think my father was trying to tell me something."

Several times after that, the painting was found in weird places around the house. It was found in the tub in the bathroom or the top shelf of the refrigerator, all the food having been relocated to other shelves as well. Muffy and her husband have never seen it move, but at least once a week it will be found sitting in a strange place in the house. The painting never leaves the house. Muffy and her husband always return the painting to its proper place in state above the fireplace.

THE SCOTT MANSION OF MERRILL, WISCONSIN

For years, people have been telling the tale of the curse put on the hill where the Scott Mansion stands in Merrill, Wisconsin.

In the 1850s, white lumbermen were moving west, cutting the virgin white pine for timber and shipping it east to be made into boats and houses and railroad timbers. As these men moved west, they would make contact with the native peoples of the area. Many of the Native Americans chose to make friendship pacts with the white men. They would trade the permission to harvest the timber for various beads and baubles from the east, as well as guns and metal combs and belt buckles. These trinkets were highly prized among the people of the villages, as anything new is among any group of people.

The lumbermen moved into an area of northern Wisconsin where the timber was especially thick and the trees huge, some towering three hundred feet or more above the needle-coated forest floor. This place seemed like a paradise to the lumbermen. There was a river nearby down which the men could float the cut timbers.

There were plenty of edible foodstuffs around to be harvested and eaten. And, there was a particularly friendly Native American tribe nearby who opened their village to the lumbermen. The men were welcomed to the area by the people of Squitee-eau-sippi, whose Indian villages extended along the Wisconsin River on what is now Merrill's west side, according to Jim Fredel of the *Wausau Daily Herald*. When the word came of the white people moving into the area, curiosity and fear warred in the people's minds. They had heard of the raids and attacks being made in Minnesota, but they also wanted the brightly colored strings of glass beads from the east. The chief of one village saw the conflict in his people and calmed their fears. The chief of the village welcomed the lumbermen, telling his people that "these men will be fair to us."

The lumbermen enjoyed talking to the villagers when they were not working. Among the villagers was the chief's daughter, given the English name of Jenny. She was a beautiful maiden and a friend to all. The chief loved her best of anything or anyone. He had refused her marriage to a young man because he could not bear to be parted from his beloved girl. She quickly made friends with the lumbermen, and they told her of the wonders of the east. She spent much time in their company, and they taught her many things. She even volunteered to be a guide to the lumbermen as they looked for the biggest stands of timber.

One fall, about a year after the lumbermen had come to the village, Jenny was sitting near the fire, and complaining that she felt cold. The chief wrapped a blanket about her shoulders, but it did not help. She fell asleep and slept for hours. When she awoke, she refused to eat or drink, saying she felt sick. Very quickly, her condition worsened, and she was too weak to even get out of bed. She died very soon after.

The chief blamed the lumbermen for the strange sickness that had robbed him of his daughter. The chief was distraught, and his despair was so deep that he called upon the Great Spirit to avenge the death of Jenny. The chief's hatred of those that had killed Jenny provoked him to utter the following curse:

> Oh, Great Spirit, grant me this place for my child. Let this ground be sacred to her memory, and let it never do any white man any good.

The Native Americans were forced out of their village and west soon after that. The land lay fallow and deserted for years. It was not until the white people began making their heavy influxes after the Civil War that the land was claimed and settled.

In 1884, T. B. Scott selected the hill for his mansion, employing an architect named Sheldon from Chicago to design it to be of surpassing beauty and opulence. During the building of the mansion, Scott, who had been in good health until then, died unexpectedly on October 7, 1886, at the age of fifty-seven. The mansion was not yet completed. Scott's wife, Ann, encouraged her son, Walter, to see that the house was completed. Within the year, Ann also passed away.

Walter Scott went to Chicago in 1887 to see the architect. Sheldon took an affront to the young man who was demanding to know why he had not yet finished the mansion that his father had commissioned. He got into an argument with Sheldon, and a fight ensued. Sheldon became enraged and advanced on Walter with the only weapon he could find. Walter was stabbed to death with a letter opener.

In 1893, a Chicago millionaire named Kuechle bought the house for a summer home. He finished the construction that had been progressing for over nine years and added his own appointments and special touches. He installed crystal chandeliers, several mantles over the mansion's many fire-places, and imported mirrors from France to grace the walls of the master suite. Several years later, Kuechle lost his fortune speculating on a California gold mine. He mortgaged the mansion for $5,000 to Chicago innkeeper Tony Barsanti. Barsanti foreclosed in 1900. Reportedly, Kuechle went insane and died in an asylum. That same year, Barsanti was stabbed in the back in Chicago's Union Station while he waited for a train to Merrill.

In 1901, George Gibson, an Illinois land speculator, bought the home from the Barsanti estate as a home for aged professional men. In August, Gibson closed his Chicago office and went to inspect the property. He was never seen or heard from again.

Mary Fehlaber, a midwife, purchased the house and thirty-nine acres of river front in 1906. She took in renters and planned to make the home into a hospital. While out riding in a horse-drawn buggy, she fell ill and went to a nearby farmhouse for help. She died before the doctor arrived.

Popcorn Dan, who served as the mansion's caretaker, traveled in 1911 to England, where he had been born. In the spring of 1912, his parents took him on a boat trip. Unfortunately, they selected the *Titanic*. He was listed as missing. After Popcorn Dan's death, a family named Lloydsen became caretakers of the mansion. Mr. Lloydsen died of alcoholism.

In all, according to reporter Fredel, nine strange deaths were associated with the hill and the mansion. In 1919, Herman Fehlhaber, the widower of Mary Fehlhaber, gave the property to the City of Merrill.

In 1923, Merrill gave the mansion and "cursed" land to the Sisters of Mercy of the Holy Cross. The condition of the sale required the sisters to establish a hospital, which they did. Reportedly the strange occurrences have stopped now that the place is a hospital.

LORI'S TALE

Lori lived on Flying Eagle Lake. She had been renting a house for about three years. Ever since the day she moved in, she had been aware of a feeling of being followed and watched. It was not a malignant feeling, it was just there. A sadness and tragedy. She would turn her head quickly and only catch a shimmer or glimpse of something.

She invited her friend to come and spend the weekend with her one day. The two women had a wonderful time, talking over old times and laughing. Lori told her friend Bonnie about all the strange happenings and about the history of the place that she had discovered. The spare bedroom—where her friend was to sleep—had been the room of a young girl who was killed in a tragic car accident.

When it was time for the women to go to sleep, they went to their rooms. Lori woke when her friend came into her room with her blanket and pillow and declared that she was not going to share a room with such a sad ghost. As she arranged herself on the floor, she told Lori that the girl had appeared seated at the desk. She kept calling for her mother and then looking out the window. Her transparent body appeared to be racked with sobs. She looked right at Lori's friend and yelled for her mother again.

Lori's friend said that she had just sat there at that desk and cried, calling for her mother and looking out the window.

The two women returned to the dark bedroom—the only light was the faint moonlight shining in the window. Together, they walked slowly toward the figure sitting at the desk. She raised her head as they approached and asked them in a hoarse whisper if they had seen her mother.

When Lori and her friend answered in the negative, she collapsed back to the desk. Her form shook with sobs again. From her throat rose the most grief-ridden howl that the two women had ever heard. It brought tears coursing from their eyes, too.

"Where is my mom?" the girl wailed.

Not knowing what to say, the women stood still and gaped at the apparition before them. This was clearly a distraught ghost. Being familiar with the mystical side of life, the two women decided to try to see if they could convince the girl that the best thing for her to do would be to "cross over." They held hands and approached the weeping girl. Speaking in soft and coaxing voices they told the girl that she would be happier to cross over. They told her that there would not be any pain like her death had caused. They told her that there would be guides that would help her find her mother and that she would be able to be reunited with her.

The ghost raised her head from the cradle of her arms and looked at them. Tears dripped from her cheeks and fell, disappearing before they reached the surface of the desk. Her hair fell limply to her shoulders. The hollowed eyes that fixed upon the two women held such a void of hope that it ached for them to look upon her. She appeared to be willing to listen to them. As the two women talked, the girl's face lost some of the grief-crazed appearance. She grew calmer and seemed to resign herself to her fate.

Slowly the flood of words from the girls ceased and they grew quiet. The pervasive silence swept in to fill the room with an almost tangible presence. The girl's face grew introspective. She regarded them with a glance that was full of sadness and gratitude at the same time. She smiled a sad smile that seemed to be full of irony.

A scratching at the door to the room caused Lori and her friend to turn. There was no critter at the door, and Lori did not have a cat or dog. No one was visible to make the noise. They looked at each other and then returned their attention to the figure at the desk.

She was gone. In the place where she had been sitting, there was a single yellow rose and a faded and creased photograph of a girl.

Lori picked up both objects and examined them. The rose was fresh, still wet from dew, and had no thorns. The picture was of the very girl that had been gracing their presence a few seconds before. She was sitting under the tree visible from the window of the room, and holding a single yellow rose.

Lori says that the place has not seemed occupied since that night. She and her friend went to bed and nothing disturbed them further.

A few months later the house was sold, the air of death and tragedy no longer pervaded.

WEREWOLF IN WISCONSIN?

Elkhorn, Wisconsin, is named as such because Colonel Samuel F. Phoenix spotted some elk horns suspended from a tree. Is it the home of the Wisconsin werewolf? The tale of the werewolf is old. The *loupe garou* from medieval French legends was supposedly a spell for magicians to turn themselves into wolves during the full moon. Quite a few movies owe their existence to the legend of the werewolf.

A werewolf is something that one can imagine in some remote forest in Eastern Europe, not something playing in a cornfield in Wisconsin. However, several responsible and reliable people have claimed to have seen a very hairy person thought to be a werewolf.

Most of the sightings have been near Bray Road where there are plenty of cornfields and woods to shelter such a beast. The accounts cover a wide spectrum, but all are similar. One person said that she saw a creature with long claws eating road kill.

The story of the werewolf has brought national recognition to the town and brought in reporters from all over the country. One reporter decided to have a sketch made from the reports given by the witness. The beast had the appearance of the classic werewolf as shown in movies and children's books.

It is worth mentioning that whether the werewolf exists or not, a person in the town of Elkhorn could find himself wearing a t-shirt sporting a picture of the Elkhorn werewolf and eating werewolf cookies from the local bakery.

STRANGE NOISES IN OAK PARK

A dinner party in Oak Park, Illinois, was continually interrupted by scratching and banging from overhead a Northwoods visitor told me. It sounded as if someone was trying to move a very heavy piece of furniture across the floor. The hostess winced every time another noise occurred. According to the host, the noises had been occurring for some time, and they had gone to look the first few times and found nothing. They had tried to find out some history of the place but so far had been unsuccessful.

The noises continued and seemed to follow the pattern of the conversation. If the chatter got louder, the noises did as well. If the noises were the topic, they would stop. The hostess seemed to be at her wits end. She looked as if she was about to crack. Her face had taken on a transparent pinched quality, as if the blood that was supposed to provide color had taken up residence somewhere else, her feet, perhaps. Her husband pressed his hand over her pale one.

Suddenly, one of the guests, who professed to be a psychic screamed "There's a gun in the house." The noises crescendoed to a fever pitch. It was a three-ring circus up there now. Thumping and banging. The sound of a glass crashing to the floor. The wife, pleading the need for fresh air, rose and left the table. Her husband dashed after her, leaving the guests in shocked silence as yet another vase was dashed to the floor overhead.

Six months later, almost to the day, the hosts sold their house. The noises had continued. It had seemed that their only option was to move away or to find therapy for the poor wife. In the process of the move, however, they went up and checked the attic again.

As they looked through the empty attic, silent for a moment, a feeling of dread and evil lured them to one corner. There was nothing there. Bare floor and roof. Upon closer inspection, it was noted that one of the floor boards was loose. With a little jiggling, the entire board lifted from its place. In a shallow cavity beneath the floor lay a gun. A thin layer of dust covered it, but it was definitely a gun— not a toy hidden by some enterprising child.

They raced down the stairs and called the police.

It was discovered that the gun had been used to commit a murder and had been hidden there by the previous owners who were friends of the murderer.

The family moved away, but there were never any more reports of noises from the attic of that house.

HALLOWEEN ON-AIR

Jim Packard hosted a Halloween show in 1995 on Wisconsin Public Radio. Listeners were encouraged to call with their own ghost stories.

One caller said she and her husband purchased an old house built in the 1800s and converted it to a suitable residence. Many times, at three in the morning, she was awakened by a radio playing the theme song from the "Little Rascals" comedy. She'd get up and look around downstairs but never found anything. There was no radio on, no television, nothing.

She had a friend and his wife visiting. The wife professed to be a psychic. "We had not told them of the strange radio-like sounds in the night," the woman told Jim Packard. Yet they, too, heard the theme from the "Little Rascals" and wondered what was going on.

The psychic told of a feeling or a sense that there was an old man in a rocking chair listening to a radio broadcast of the "Little Rascals." "He loves to listen to the radio," she said.

71

Other happenings in the house included the breaking of ash trays. It remains, as do the radio stories, an unsolved mystery.

Halloween 1996

Larry Meiller had another round of Halloween fun in 1996. The strangest call a listener made into the show was from a Green Bay resident telling about a moment when he was sixteen. He was seated on the porch with a girlfriend. "It was 9:00 P.M. I looked at her, and her face contorted, making the strangest expression I ever saw." He said that another friend committed suicide soon afterwards and knows in his heart there was a connection.

And how about ghost cows? A caller told about a herd of Brown Swiss ghost cows spotted on a lime ridge in Richland County, complete with a ghost farmer trying to milk them.

One caller said she walked a Wisconsin arboretum in 1972 and heard wood being chopped. There was little mistaking the sound—the thunk of the axe into the trunk in slow, steady rhythm. There was even a tree felled but no footprints in the snow. The caller said it was later when she discovered that farmers who had lived on the property some one hundred years earlier had also made notations about the strange sound of someone chopping wood.

Larry Meiller told a tale about one of his Wisconsin Public Radio colleagues. The story goes that this person and a friend had been walking out west on an old deserted trail when they came to a fork in the path and did not know which way to go. They saw an older couple walking up the hill in front of them. They were dressed, not as hikers, but in regular clothing of fifty or sixty years before. The older couple spoke to them, telling them to take the left trail and not the one to the right. The hikers followed the advice and took the left fork of the trail. Later, at the end of the trail, they were told by others how lucky they were to have taken the trail they had and not the other, which was wiped out in a flash flood.

Ride on the Radio Waves

This story is of a ghost named Sophie haunting an old mansion. The children who lived in the creaky old building used a Ouija board and made contact with Sophie. She told them of the former head servant, Larry Alden, who had worked there. That was later verified. Sophie said she often took the form of an old woman sitting in a rocking chair that could be seen through the parlor window when kids came around looking for scares. She'd turn and glare at them, revealing her big teeth. Apparently spirits still have some fun in our world.

THROUGH A CHILD'S EYES

Sue from Madison, Wisconsin, said her young grandson, Michael, was the only one who saw a spirit known as Matthew.

"He first saw Matthew when he was in his crib and started talking with him," Sue said. "Once, Julie, Michael's mother, said his big-wheel bike was in the kitchen when all of a sudden, it rolled to the front door. Thinking the floor slanted, Julie placed Michael's ball in the same spot. It didn't move.

"Another time, they were entering a room when Michael stopped and said. 'Can't do that. Ghost won't let me.' That startled all of them because they couldn't remember ever having used the word 'ghost' around Michael."

Sue added, "They found an old photo in the house. It showed three people, one of which was a young boy wearing a long, white dress. Michael pointed to it and said, 'Matthew.' No one could verify or deny that the child went by that name.

One day, while Michael was playing with his toys on the floor in his room, the lights started flickering. For a few seconds, they flickered, and then they just went out. After checking the bulbs, Julie went downstairs to the fuse box to see if that was the problem. The blown fuse to Michael's room was labeled, "Matthew's Room."

The family only stayed in the haunted house for some six weeks before moving on. Michael never said if Matthew followed them.

GHOSTLY VISITORS AND EERIE CHARM

Charles Pfister dreamed of a hotel on a grand scale in the West that would be visited by the eastern socialites and be well-renown for its wondrous appointments. In the late part of the nineteenth century, his dream was realized in the Pfister Hotel. The "Grand Hotel of the West" was the pinnacle of comfort and luxury in the rough and tumble West. Complete with a grand ballroom, sweeping staircases, and polished copper touches on the fixtures, the Pfister was truly a sight to be seen, and Charles presided over it like a king. Guests would see him at the head of the table at meal times, or in his favorite chair in the study with a book and a pipe in hand.

The Pfister was everything that Charles wanted it to be. It was renown even on the East Coast. A veritable army of maids, bellhops, and cookstaff kept the place spotless, convenient, and the patrons well-fed.

During his tenure there, Charles made sure that the hotel was running as close to perfection as possible. His every day was spent prowling the building and grounds, seeing to every imaginable need of his guests. He spent every remaining day of his life doing what he loved best. When he did pass, he was celebrated and mourned. However, the story does not end there.

Since his death, guests have reported seeing a man roaming the halls and open places of the hotel. His intentions seem to be to make sure that his life's work remains the way he envisioned it. He has been spotted surveying the lobby from the grand staircase, strolling the minstrel's gallery above the ballroom and passing through the ninth-floor storage area. He is always described in the same way, "older," "portly," "smiling," and "well-dressed."

The grand portrait of Charles Pfister still graces the main lobby, above the big fireplace mantel. Upon seeing a portrait of Pfister, witnesses swear that it was that very man they had seen. No doubt, well-tended regular customers say that if this visitor is Charles Pfister, he is a most welcomed guest indeed.

MINNESOTA TOWN FULL OF HAUNTS

Lanesboro, Minnesota, is a sleepy town that sits on the bluffs of the Root River in southern Minnesota. The residents seem to be plagued by many strange occurrences. It is a pretty town that holds many secrets.

Farms are very common in that area, the land is fertile and rich. However, one family living there seems to be infested with mischievous spirits. It is awfully hard to get work done when one is constantly searching for tools. Tools are carefully placed in their proper places, and the next thing anyone knows, they have moved to another location entirely. Once or twice, this could be chalked up to forgetfulness or misplacing the tool, but this happens constantly. The farm workers never know where a tool is going to show up. It is not just small hand tools, either. Larger pieces of equipment are found missing all the time. Sometimes, during planting, a wrench or hammer is found in the fields. Sometimes, tools are found in buildings where they never were before. Residents of the farm swear that this has gone on for years. Some say that it is a group of fun-loving ghosts, but critics say it is just kids playing jokes on the trusting owners.

The Root River meanders through the lush farmland, creating absolutely breathtaking bluffs and vistas. However, one bluff is avoided by human life as much as possible. The bluff top is wracked by the disembodied screams of a child. It is said that there was once a shanty up there, over 150 years ago. A young mother lived there with her child. Her husband had volunteered for the Civil War and was killed at the battle of Mill Springs. The young woman decided to try to raise her son on her own rather than face the long and dangerous journey back east. She worked her land and bartered for what she could not make or grow. For several years, life was hard, but they survived.

Winter was cold, and much of it was spent with just enough food to stave off starvation but never enough to be completely full. The threadbare clothes they both wore never kept them from the chilblains caused by the bitter wind. There was not quite enough wood to make the shanty warm and most of the heat escaped through the cracks in the walls no matter how patched the tar paper was. Blizzards would roar out of the northwest and bury the shanty in snow so deep they were stuck until they could crawl out a window and dig out the front door. They were alone in an unforgiving environment, one that did not allow mistakes.

Winter eventually gave way to spring, however hesitantly. Spring to summer and summer to fall. The years cycled around, moving from times of backbreaking labor to times of cabin fever so strong that even the frozen prairie seemed a better alternative.

One late summer the cycle finally ended. The young mother left her son, who was about four by this point, asleep in the cabin and set out to cut firewood for the impending winter. The river bluffs were full of deadfalls and timber that could be cut. The warm day was clear and bright. The leaves were starting to take on the late summer yellow tinge that signified the oncoming fall and winter. Flocks of birds were swirling in shimmering clouds through the trees, and the grasses were the baked golden-brown of early fall. There would be few days left like this before another confining winter set in. With her axe set over her shoulder, and a mule to help haul the wood up to the shanty she set out, heading down into the bluffs.

Birds chattered to each other and the new-fallen leaves crunched beneath her boots. The placid mule's steady gait followed her, pausing now and then to rip up a mouth full of grass and chew meditatively on it. She moved from deadfall to deadfall, looking for one dry enough for winter use. The wind sang through the trees and made her skirts billow and dance around her ankles. The beauty of the day and the chance to be alone with her own thoughts made her smile—something she had almost forgotten how to do. Splashes of color glimmered up from the river bank where stands of sumac were donning their fiery fall finery.

The bluff looked, for a few seconds, like the hills around Boston where she was raised. She made her way to the bottom of the bluff to get a drink of water. The river sparkled in the sunlight. She set her axe down and ground tethered the mule so that he too could drink. She gathered her skirts and hopped to a rock surrounded by the clear, cold water. Bending over, she cupped a mouthful in her hand and drank. The cool water, sweet and fresh, slid down her throat and she stood for a moment as the droplets caught the sunlight as they fell back to the river. The mule slurped water noisily behind her. She watched fish move in the water and watched a great blue heron spear a fish with its long pointed bill. Content in the moment of peace she had, she stepped back to the shore. Her boots slipped on the slick rocks and she stumbled back into the edge of the river. She caught herself before she landed up to her waist in the water, but managed to scrape herself on the sharp rocks lining the bank. More carefully, she climbed out of the river and pulled herself onto the bank. She grabbed the mule's reins and started the long climb back up the bluff to the deadfall she had decided was the driest. Her now sodden boots slipped and skidded over the rocks protruding from the bluff.

Suddenly, the characteristic rattle of the timber rattlesnake sounded from a sunny rock. She had disturbed him where he was sunning himself. Startled by the snake, she stepped back abruptly. Her boots slipped on the rock, and she tumbled head over heels back down the cliff. Her violent passing knocked several large rocks loose, and they rumbled after her. The mule started too, and ran headlong up the bluff and home.

The young mother and the loosened boulders tumbled to the bottom of the bluff. After the boulders splashed to a rest in the river, her body lay broken and bleeding on a smooth flat rock ledge—one hand dangling in the water with a trickle of blood dripping into the river. Her eyes did not see the birds that were flocking in the trees over her head, and never again would her small son feel her tender caresses in the night.

The boy awoke several hours later, almost at dusk and looked for his mother. She had admonished him never to climb down the bluff without her, so he roamed the top of the bluff calling for her. She never answered. He died not too many days later, and wildflowers grew up where his body lay. It is his voice that is said to still roam, just as the sun touches the tops of the hills with rose-tinged light, looking for the mother who could never again answer her small son.

Another tale that has been told of the area is that of a young woman who has been seen for centuries paddling her birch bark canoe down the river, all the while singing a haunting song.

The heat of the prairie rose in shimmering waves and hung in the air. Hapless gusts of wind drifted listlessly across the rolling hills. The sweet scent of wildflowers and the brown smell of grasses mingled with the the cool damp from the river bottoms pulling the smoke from the cook-fires into a dance that sang of summer.

The village was humming with quiet activity, every person busy at their assigned task. Strips of buffalo dried on racks and fishes pulled from the river hung out of the reach of the dogs that whined for a taste. Quiet chatter floated over the groups that were seated around working on various projects: buckskin garments, and chewing the sinews used to tie the bark huts together. Everyone was busy and talking, even children moved in groups with the work set to them by watchful parents and guardians. Only one person was missing from the quiet community of workers.

Killdeer ran, escaping the tedious chores that left her arms aching to be in the cool water of the river. She let the wind run its tender fingers through her unbound hair. She moved through the forest, dodging trees and jumping snags. Her feet felt light and unhindered. The glimpses of blue sky that peeked through the green canopy that arched overhead reflected down in the river and sparkled through the brown of the trunks. Moss grew over the fallen trunks and rocks. Birds twittered companionably to her as she passed, and occasionally a startled squirrel would scold her from a branch high in an oak tree. The white flash of a deer's tail would be the only thing she saw as she passed. She ran flat out until her hot feet splashed into the cool current of the river. Sand, disturbed by her abrupt entrance, settled around her ankles.

She pulled her deerskin jerkin off over her head and tossed it into a careless heap on the river bank. Then with a deep breath she dove into the cool depths of the river. The current was strong here, but she battled it and gloried in the way the cool water caressed her bare skin. Her long hair, black as the sky at midnight, flowed about her like honey moving this way and that by the power of the currents and ripples. Her strong arms pulled her sleek body through the water, sending drops high into the air with each stroke. The sun felt warm on her head as she swam. After swimming for a while, she felt cooler. She swam to one of the rocky ledges that extended out over the water, and pulled herself out of the cool greenish water of the pool out of the current that formed there. She sat on the rock, her hair pouring down her back.

The shade allowed breaths of breeze to dry the water from her body. She sat on the rock watching the water flow past her, mesmerized. The peace of the area always infused her, making her calm and serene. She gathered her knees up to her chest and rested her head on them. The sunlight glinted on the little wavelets that the currents created. A fish leaped. Bugs skittered across the water's surface. The hum of life around her lulled her into sleep.

She did not hear the hush that crept over the river bottom. The silence of the animals did not penetrate her dreams. She slept on until a chill stole over her and she stirred. Coming to a sudden awareness that she was not alone, she dashed for the spot where her jerkin had landed. Just as she reached it, the bushes near the rock where she had slept stirred. Two yellowed eyes glared at her from between some leaves. She moved from the jerkin and dove into the river. She swam to the middle where the current was the swiftest before turning to view the owner of the yellowed eyes.

A man unfolded himself from the bushes and strolled with a false nonchalance toward the bank. His leather tunic and trews were stained and torn. They hung from his frame as if they were made for a much bigger man. His long hair was matted and hung about his shoulders in untidy clumps. His face was seamed with scars, and bruises lined his jaw. His expression contorted into a mixture of a scowl and a proprietary glint that repulsed and terrified her. She turned and swam as fast as she could for the other bank. A loud splash followed her movement. He was coming after her. She added an extra burst of speed to her stroke and reached the shore. She pulled herself onto the grassy bank and slid up. She stood and ran, getting out of sight before he could swim across. She circled around to a bend in the river and plunged back in, swimming to the other bank again. Once she reached the other bank, she pulled herself out of the water and sprinted back to the place where her jerkin lay in the mud of the bank.

She grabbed her jerkin and pulled it on over her head. A small sound, the raining of droplets into the water, behind her made her whirl around. The man stood before her, a sadistic grin on his face with rows of teeth, rotten in their sockets, exposed. He backhanded her, and she fell to the ground stunned. The last sight she saw was his cruel face bending over her prone form as he dropped his trews. Then darkness claimed her.

When she awoke, the man was gone. Her face felt hot and puffed where he had hit her, and her legs were purpling. Blood trickled down from between her legs. Dirt was smeared over her body, and the foul stench of the man seemed to be in her very pores. She plunged into the river again and scrubbed her body with sand. She rubbed and rubbed, trying to get her skin to calm down. The thought of what he had done to her made her skin crawl. She gathered up the remains of her jerkin and began the arduous climb up the bluff. It was dark now, the sun having gone to bed during her wit-wandering.

When she reached the top of the bluff, after stumbling into trees, her body was shaking from cold and reaction.

She saw the ground rising up to meet her again, but strong arms caught her as she fell into another faint.

When she awoke finally, she was in her own bed in her father's hut. The healer was chanting in the corner and the air smelled strongly of herbs. Her father sat near her, watching for some sign of movement and the return to consciousness. The sight of him caused tears to flow over her mal-treated cheeks. She longed to throw herself into his arms as she had done so often as a child, but she hurt so much that she could not move. Her very being seemed to be rebelling from her will power.

"I'm sorry, Father," she whispered.

"Killdeer, my poor girl, how did you get into such a pass?" her father asked as he moved closer to her. He enveloped her in an embrace, and she collapsed against his shoulder, consumed by sobs. Slowly, the entire story came out, how she ran off from her chores and went swimming, and how she fell asleep on the rock, awaking when she sensed his presence. She told him everything. He listened to her quietly, and then, when she fell into a natural sleep, he left her. Within a few hours, the animal that had raped his daughter lay in the dust before the chief of the tribe. It sniveled and whined, but his ears heard it not. With a single barked command, the man-animal lay dead before him.

It took a long time for Killdeer to heal; like her namesake she was a loner, seeking the solace of the woods when the chatter and bustle of the village overwhelmed her. Another change was progressing, marked by the slow but steady swelling of her belly.

All through the winter, Killdeer marked the passage of time by the expanding of her belly, and, when in the spring a baby boy was born to her, she healed. She named the baby for the river. She loved him, though he sprang from great distress, he came with great joy to her. She and her son continued to live in the house of her father. The family engulfed the new mother and her child and filled her with love and support. Killdeer showed her son the land around them that had given her so much comfort. She bathed him in the river, and together they sat in the sunlight and watched the baby deer come to drink from the swift water with their mothers. River grew. Killdeer glowed at each new milestone, reveling as her son learned to walk and talk. Every day they would go on long walks together and Killdeer would talk to him or sing lullabies to him. One such lullaby was a particularly beautiful and haunting song that spoke of the river and the life that flowed there. Killdeer took River with her wherever she went.

One day, when River was about eighteen months old, Killdeer took him in a canoe down the river to gather wild rice. Killdeer settled River in the canoe and stepped nimbly in. She sat down in the rear of the canoe to paddle. The canoe cut through the water smoothly, and with each strong stroke the canoe sped on further. She watched River sitting, playing with his puppet.

The river was running high from recent rains, and it moved quickly. There was a small rapids that she had to run before the river widened into the marshy area where the rice grew. She was a good canoe handler, and had run the rapids many times before. As the roar of water started to reach her ears, she realized how high the river was running. River heard it and looked alarmed. She sang his song to him to quiet him, and returned her attention to the rapids. The river, narrow and deep, moving very quickly. Water rushed through the canyon. A wave swept over the bow, soaking River. Another came, sweeping away his doll. He was crying now, a shriek that rivaled the river in volume. Killdeer could not leave her paddle or the canoe would be dashed to the rocks. Suddenly, another wave came and the canoe tipped sharply to one side. River slid. Another wave, closely following, swept him into the roiling water. Killdeer sprang forward, but River was ripped from her grip as the river shook him like a dog shaking a rat. She dove into the rapids after him, but he was gone.

Hours later, at sunset, she was found holding his small lifeless body in the shallows of the marsh. The song she was crooning was more than the simple lullaby now, she poured all her grief and sadness into the words. The voice that poured from her throat was no longer sane. As the men sent to help her tried to remove River from her arms, a scream ripped from her chest that made the hair on the back of their necks stand on end. The men took her gently back to the village, but within a few days she was gone. Footsteps led to the river bank. Her body was never found.

Every evening since then, she has been seen paddling up and down the river singing the song that River had loved so much and crooning her sorrow to the little one she could not live without.

Another tale to come out of Laneboro:

In the 1870s, the railroad was the only means of communication with the rest of the world for people living in small towns like Lanesboro. Trains came through the town regularly, bringing mail, news, and visitors. The engineers on the trains had to be competent men who could watch for blockage on the track that could derail a train. It was these men who spotted a man.

It may seem an odd occurrence for a train to toot its horn whenever it rounds a certain bend in the track outside of Lanesboro, but, until the last train passed through the town in 1973, that is exactly what happened.

As often as not a man would be standing on the track as the train passed, seemingly running him over, but if the train slowed and someone got out to check, there would be no sign of the body, or anybody. The man has stood on the track for over one hundred years, appearing in the evening when the train came through. He would not move, he would just calmly raise his hand in a futile attempt to signal the train to stop. The first few times the man appeared, the engineer ground on the brakes and brought the train to a stop, but after several occurrences of this, they just tooted the horn and moved on through.

Legend has it that in the mid-1800s a boy drowned in the river below the tracks. A man who had found him, raced to the top of the cliff, hoping that he could find help from one of the white men that had settled in the area. No help was forthcoming. The boy was dead.

Every evening since then — over one hundred years — the man has stood in the path of the trains, signaling them to stop and help.

Lanesboro is the home of many strange happenings, and many of them are sad, but it is still a beautiful little town on the bluffs of the Root River.

LADY CATHERINE'S STRANGE ENCOUNTER

Lady Catherine told of the burial of her father. She had been a daddy's girl in every sense of the word. "I loved him dearly," she said, "but I felt his spirit was still among us even at the funeral." She did not want to accept that he was dead. To her, the motions of the funeral seemed mechanical. Like dance steps. It all swirled around her, and she kept watching for her father to come and make everything all better.

Lady Catherine said that even after the ceremony, she, too, like his spirit, refused to let him go to his just reward. His spirit, she said, was concerned that she did not want him to go. As she stood at the graveside, she felt the warring emotions in her, but refused to acknowledge what she knew to be true. Instead, she stared resolutely at the raw hole in the ground. After the interment, she turned and began to walk away.

"I had my back to the graveside and started to walk away. Just then, a large flame scorched my back. I jumped and yelped, looking back quickly. There was no flame, and the people at the graveside stared at me in bewilderment. They hadn't seen anything. Yet, right at that moment, I knew it was my father cutting loose and telling me to get on with my life. There had been a flame, and I had felt intense heat." She could even smell the ozone in the air. Her memories of her father comforted her, but also the knowledge that she had let him go on to his reward.

A STRANGENESS AT BOOK WORLD IN HAYWARD

Jeanine Sill told me about a certain strange happening in the store.

"Sometimes I look around to see if someone is smoking a pipe," Jeanine said, "and there'd be no one there. It only happens at certain times—that distinct smell of a man's pipe."

Whoever was smoking that fragrant tobacco got a stern warning from Jeanine anyway. "Don't burn the books!"

Jeanine told me about a time when she and a friend were in New Auburn, Wisconsin, on a windy and dark night. "We walked by this old house and decided to go in. It was a shambles—even the lath was showing in the walls. Oddly, there were cow hoof print marks all throughout the structure. The place looked like a haunted house to us, and we left."

"We returned the following night." It was a windy night and the old house creaked and groaned as it swayed. That time they saw a light in the vacated house. On the second floor, which was doubly odd, because the rotted wood could not have held any weight on the second floor. It was so windy that it could not have been a candle or any other means of flame. "There was no way any light could be on in that old place; the wiring was out. And what we saw was real electric lights, or so it seemed. Needless to say, we increased our pace—out!—and we never went back."

JOSIE OF EAGLE RIVER AND OTHER TALES

The Polish Grandmother

Prior to a talk at the Walter Olson Library in Eagle River, Wisconsin, a gentleman named Rich told me a most bizarre story about his grandmother, Josie, whom he affectionately called "my Polish grandmother."

"One day she had the most beautiful black hair you ever saw," he told me. "The next day, however, her hair had all turned white. I was shocked and, of course, asked her what had happened.

"She then told me a story of what had happened to her during her sleep. She had seen a man in a bright white light—in her bedroom. She said it was her son, Norman.

"I didn't know that name or that uncle. Later the family revealed that he had been killed decades before in a car crash in 1948 on Highway 45 north of Eagle River. . . . Drag racing was just starting as a fad in those years, and he was doing that when he was killed. Apparently, grandmother's dead son had appeared to her that night and so frightened her that her hair had turned from black to white.

"The next day, still very agitated about the whole experience, she made me walk all the way from her home to the old Ford garage just to look at the death car still stored there."

Sighting at Lake Jaclyn

His name is George Friedrich, and he lives on a small lake, Jaclyn, in Wisconsin's Portage County. According to him, his lake has been visited by several UFOs every year.

"One six-foot, round large ball came from over there," he said, pointing to some trees half a mile or so to the right of his pier. "They're so frequent that it's no big deal anymore."

A Sense of Healing at Mann Lake

One Thursday, Don Wojnowskis, one of a fairly large group of two families up from Chicago, stopped by the main house to chat. We got to talking about strange happenings in the area. We swapped tales for a bit, and as he was walking back to his camp, he confided, "I better not tell the others about this stuff."

Two days later, the small army left for the rigors of the six-hour trek back to Chicago. The next day I received a call from Franz Perfect, head of the other family group. "By the way, something happened on Friday night (August 14)."

He explained that Danny, the fifteen-year-old mentally-challenged son of the Wojnowskis, had had something very strange happen to him.

"We were talking on the way home in the car, and Danny started telling us about this strange thing that happened last night. It seems in the middle of the night Danny had a severe case of back spasms. He told my daughter Jennifer about it, but she didn't think to ask anything of what followed.

"Danny said he felt a hand on his back, and there was an energy—a heat force, if you will. The back spasms

94

ended at once. Danny told Jennifer he thought it was the hand of God."

I suppose it might have been the hand of God, but with all the stories of Sven appearing in that guest cabin, I'm not so sure. But whatever it was, the boy's back was better and it was no drug that did that.

Sven was a ghost who had appeared in that guest cabin for years. I never told a person about the tales until they came to me and told me of their experiences. In this way I knew that Sven was real.

Ray Smallish, Jr., who had helped to remodel that guest cabin, and I talked a bit about the old cabin on Mann Lake, and I mentioned that it was haunted.

Ray stopped thumbing through his magazine and looked at me, not saying anything. After a moment, he said quietly, "When Joe Lisner and I were working on the cabin, we saw things. We'd be in the cabin, and out of the corner of our eyes — both of us — we'd see people. We'd turn quickly, and they'd be gone. We'd both look at each other, not saying anything, but knowing that each had seen the apparition, we'd start working again.

"Then it would happen again. People. We'd turn, and they'd be gone. That quick. Can't even describe them. Don't know if they were men or women, but they were people. We both finally talked about it. Old Joe just shook his head and continued to work.

"We saw them again and again all during that week. We weren't afraid or anything, but we knew they were ghosts. And, yes, I do believe in ghosts."

ART HELLYER SEES SOMETHING STRANGE

Art Hellyer was driving down Highway 7, late one night. It was a clear night and a nearly full moon illuminated the road and surrounding area clearly. It was a cold night; late October usually is in the Northwoods. The heater was working overtime to keep the cabin of his car toasty, and Art was singing along to the oldies station. He had a few more miles to go before he would get home to his warm bed and sleep. It had been a long day. He had been on the phone all morning trying to line up guests for his annual Halloween radio show. A day of busy signals and answering machines had left him frustrated and tired.

He rolled down the window a crack and lit a cigarette. The cherry-red tip glowed brightly in the semi darkness. He glanced in the rearview mirror, his face lit up in the red-orange light. As he ashed out the window, the sparks caught in the wind and danced along the smooth tar of the road. There was no one on the road this late on such a cold night. Trees reached bony hands across the road overhead, casting eery shadows from the moonlight. Art could feel the cold air flowing in the window, like water in a flood. He shivered and tossed the butt out the window.

Rolling up the window, he pulled himself out of a comfortable slouch. Another glance in the rearview revealed no more than the road behind him. The beams of his headlights lit on some leaves that were blowing across the road in a sudden gust of wind. Art watched the trees pick up the swaying and dancing of the leaves as the wind gusted through the tops. There were few leaves left on them, but the near-naked branches tossed. Death reaching up out of the grave to grab him. Art shivered again. He shook his head to clear out those thoughts. All day talking to people who are ghost experts and spookologists, he was starting to crack. *Besides, who really believed in ghosts anymore?*

Just as those thoughts were brushing the inside of his skull with the unbidden shivers that they conjured up, something caught his attention. A girl in a lacy white dress was walking through the graveyard. She was moving slowly, in no hurry as he would be if he were out in the cold. She walked methodically, and with a purpose. Art slowed his car. *No one should be out on a night like this.* As he watched, the girl walked through the cast iron bars of the fence surrounding the cemetery and walked across the road.

Art slammed on the brakes when it looked like he was going to hit her, leaving black streaks that shone in the moonlight. His car swerved from his aggressive deceleration, and for a moment his attention was occupied by getting the car back under control. When he had pulled the car to a stop, he looked up. He had not hit her, he would have heard and felt that, so she must be behind him. He looked in the mirror. No girl. He craned his head around, but still saw nothing. He put the car in park and opened the door. Cold air flooded around him and he drew in a sharp breath. Exhaling, his breath hung in the air for a few seconds before another gust of wind carried it away. Bundling his coat around his body, he stood up and shut the door to keep as much heat in as possible. He walked along the road, looking for the glow of the white dress in the moonlight, hoping some movement would betray her hiding place. Nothing. Further investigation still revealed nothing. It was as if the girl had not existed.

Later, when he was back in his car, as Aretha Franklin declared that she needed respect on the radio, only then did it occur to him that not only had she disappeared from sight in the space of a few seconds, but she had walked through the solid metal bars of the fence. She had not gone over and she had not hesitated before them, just walked through as if they were not there.

Shaken, he slowly put the car in drive and went home. Somehow his bed had never looked more inviting.

THE HURLEY MYSTERY OF LOTTA MORGAN

A woman named Lotta Morgan lived in Hurley, Wisconsin, during the late 1800s. She was married to a man who treated her badly so she packed up and left one day. She moved to Milwaukee where she got a job waiting tables at one of the local hotels. There she met a man who was a Pinkerton detective. She spent a great deal of time with him, giving rise to the rumors that she was an agent. She worked until she earned enough money to go west and find a new life for herself. She left in the night, as was her pattern by now. She moved north and west, going deep into the Northwoods and the Iron Range in Minnesota. She moved from town to town, working briefly in inns and taverns, but the women disapproved of her, and the men only wanted to bed her. Winter was about to set in, and her options were quickly dwindling. She had to find a place to hole up or she faced conditions for which her life in the city had done nothing to prepare her.

She discovered that she could make a place for herself in the lumbercamps of northern Minnesota. Many of the men there were not only single but were facing a long cold winter without the possibility of being with a woman. Lotta used the skills she had learned and was quickly much in demand. She spent several years working and living in the camps, but she eventually got an urge to move on again.

After she left the camps, she apparently moved around a great deal. Nothing is known about her until several years later.

In 1890, Lotta Morgan was found murdered in an alley in Hurley. An axe was found imbedded in her skull. All her jewelry was on her body and money still lay in her purse. There was no sign of a struggle except that the small pistol that she carried was found some three feet from her body.

Her apartment across from the Exchange Bank may have revealed some information about a plot to murder Hurley's finest citizen, or so a local myth purported. However, nothing was ever really known. No one knew anything for sure.

The Hurley myth also stated that many in the lively city knew who killed Lotta all those years ago, but the information was kept close to the vest, supposedly until the heirs of the villains passed.

When the Roofer Heard "Woof, Woof"

Eddie lives in Presque Isle with his prized German shepherd. He began to hear strange sounds coming from under his house. They sounded like growls, scratchings, and other animal noises. Each time he looked, however, he saw nothing. The growls continued, especially late in the night. Threats from him failed to quiet the sounds. He considered firing a gun under the house, but animal lover that he was, he couldn't give that serious thought. What he did do was take the gun outside, cock it and threaten to fire it. He called out to the mysterious beasts — or beings — telling them that, if they didn't move on, he would surely fire the gun. That night, blissful silence. His bluff had worked. Whatever had been making the strange animal noises, it seems, understood him and sought a safer location for haunting.

"Now, Cut That Out . . ."

Radio comedian Jack Benny made the line, "Now, cut that out!" part of American culture, but a friend in Manitowish Waters, Wisconsin, yelled the line frequently to a ghost named Josephine, who did strange things to her fire.

The friend, who lived on Spider Lake, said the ghost of Josephine liked to play with the fire and the logs in her fireplace.

"Sometimes she'll make a log last all night," she said. "Other times she'll make the fire flare up and then die down and then flare up again. It's really crazy."

She explained that Josephine was "ticked" that she was "screwed out of the home" by a con artist after she and her boyfriend saved all their money to build their dream home on Spider Lake. "They were from Chicago. Josephine and her friend had worked for the McCormicks. When it came time for the big move, they found that they had been conned out of the deal. They lost everything."

Josephine died some time later and moved right into the Spider Lake home as a ghost. She been there ever since, and she's still ticked.

GANGSTERS

Gangsters roamed these thick lush Northwoods in the 1920s and 1930s. They took a respite from the Chicago scene in the pine woods and cool waters. Resort owners knew about the love the guys and their molls had for these places and, for the most part, the resorts were a haven for them. Even today, though the Roaring Twenties are long over, the gangsters seem to roam these wild places where they were accepted so many years ago.

Little Bohemia in Manitowish Waters, Wisconsin, is a place well known for the fact the gangster John Dillinger escaped from there in 1934. It was really the beginning of the end for Dillinger. J. Edgar Hoover was so angry that the capture of the Public Enemy Number One was botched so badly—resulting in the death of one civilian and the injury of two others—that he ordered a massive manhunt. When Dillinger was killed not too much later, it saved the reputation of the fledgling FBI.

Little Bohemia is a resort built on Little Star Lake. Dillinger and some of his gang spent some time there in

1934, and with a tip from the owner, a capture was staged to bring him in. Dillinger escaped to the serenade of machine gun fire behind him. Four months later he was dead upon a sidewalk in Chicago.

Little Bohemia is rumored to be haunted. One of the waitresses, who stayed in the same bedroom that Dillinger inhabited, claims that she has heard footsteps coming down an empty hallway. One day, she even saw a transparent man slinking down the hallway carrying a gun.

St. Paul, Minnesota, was well known to harbor criminals during the height of the gangster era. Criminals had to pay a small fee and register with the local police, then they were able to roam the city without worry of arrest. Everyone was welcome: criminals, escapees, and ex-cons. St. Paul gathered them all in and protected them. Is it any wonder that to a city known to have protected them in life, the gangsters would flock in death.

The Castle Royal, the world's first underground nightclub, was constructed in sandstone caves in the cliffs of St. Paul in 1933. Previous to housing the night club, it held food for the city, because it stayed at a perfect fifty-two degrees all the time; then some enterprising souls started a mushroom growing business in the caves, which prospered for many years. After that Josie Lehman, daughter of the owners, decided that the cave would be better serving as a swanky night club for the criminal clientele that flocked to St. Paul. The club was a fantastic success. It soon became a favorite haunt of Ma Barker and John Dillinger, as well as many other lesser-known toughs. One of the first occurrences of strange happenings was in 1934 when the club was empty except for a cleaning lady. As she walked into the main room of the club, she found herself in the middle of a full-blown gun battle between three men. Machine gun bullets were zinging everywhere. She dropped to the ground and made her way to the phone where she called the police. However, due to the corruption of the police during that period of St. Paul's history, it took over an hour and a half for them to arrive. They came upon a scene where there were no bodies, no blood, no guns; however, there were real bullet holes in the soft sandstone of the walls and ceiling. The holes remain to this day.

Over the years, many other tales have surfaced from the caves, tales of noises heard where they cannot be explained such as glasses clinking, or voices, or gunfire. The shady history of the caves manifests itself in ghostly apparitions that appear at three in the morning. A man and a woman occupy a booth, whisper and chat with each other, and then disappear.

St. Paul offered sanctuary to the mob and other criminals in a time when the world saw them as heros, the stuff of legends. Now, the legends have created themselves as the caves offer sanctuary to the long-dead gangsters once again. The current owners of the caves have opened their doors to the ghosts, and so once again the boys and their sexy molls roam the haunts of St. Paul.

UFO SiGHTiNGS

Guy Collins told a story about one strange night in St. Paul when he was a student at the University of St. Thomas many years before. "We were in the barracks for the night," he said, explaining that, at the time, St. Thomas students had to go through Air Force training as part of the curriculum, including staying in barracks and wearing uniforms. "We were listening to the radio, and one station stated that there was a UFO in the southwest sky of the Twin Cities. [I got up] and walked to the window at the end of the hall. I looked southwest, and I did see a big light. It glowed red and green. I really didn't believe it, didn't believe that UFOs actually existed, but I couldn't deny I was seeing something I surely didn't understand. The light remained in the sky for some ten minutes. All my roommates saw it, too.

"Then it disappeared. Just like that. Suddenly we saw it again near the horizon in a different part of the sky. In half a second, I'd guess it traveled some 300 miles. It was truly an unbelievable experience."

Julie McPeek, said that she, too, had a UFO tale. "It was in the Madison area," she said. "At first I didn't see it . . . I felt it. I felt an enormous pressure. I knew something was above me. I looked up. It was a craft with three angles, like a triangle, and it was red. There were five white lights circling it. I could not hear a thing, but I sure could feel its weight. Then it moved away, heading north."

Those Fried Green Ghosts of Galena

The old and very poor farm that housed the sick and mentally ill (from 1870 through the Depression years) is now called Fried Green Tomatoes Country Italian Restaurant. There are rumors of many strange things happening there.

"A spoon stands upright with no help at times," said waitress Lea Droessler, but she confided that most of the strange happenings occurred on the third floor where the mentally disabled were housed.

While the restaurant was closed for the night "a line of salt has been found on the floor when no one was in the building. People are always tripping on the third step leading to the third floor. The plates that adorn the strange-looking light fixtures were all turned around one morning. A state trooper who occasionally stopped by late at night to check things out reportedly saw reaching figures in the windows of the third floor."

Just to make things particularly interesting, right across the road from the restaurant is the place where it is said the only hanging ever in Jo Davies County took place.

Shadows from the Past

Paul Eck of Park Falls, Wisconsin, told a strange story of a photograph taken by a friend of his. This friend, having served in Europe during World War II, returned and visited Dachau, the Nazi concentration camp where thousands of Jews were killed. "When my friend took a picture of the gate, something strange showed up when the film was developed," Paul said. "Right at the entrance was the image of a Nazi guard. We had the photo and negative checked, and the photo people could not explain what had happened."

That's Earl, Brother

Earl Einer, former Woodruff, Wisconsin, town chairman and its longtime police chief, told of an amazing UFO story. He said he saw the UFO years before over Highway 51 north of town. It was "a big silver thing" that just hovered over the highway. It hung in the air for several minutes, before shooting into the sky and disappearing among the stars.

Strange Happenings in Eagle River

"My friend Bob and his two children were here from Traverse City, Michigan," said Ginny, a waitress in Eagle River. "We were out watching the lights at Watersmeet. It was a very dark night, and I was lying on the hood of the car."

"I noticed that way up [in the sky] was this blackness where I could see no stars, nothing. Out of the blackness came two objects, one right after another. They went this way and that. I called out to Bob to look, and he too saw them. He couldn't believe his eyes. They darted this way and that at great speeds. It was truly frightening and yet inspiring at the same time."

THE HOUSE IN ONTONOGON

A woman told the following story:

The house my husband and I bought in Ontonogon, Michigan, was built in 1927 and remained with the original family until August 1992, when we moved in. Almost immediately, strange things began to happen. Banging against the front door, lights turning off by themselves, doors opening and closing, heavy objects falling from the air, crashing to the floor with nothing to account for how that could happen, a tangible presence.

All of this has been very frightening. My husband works out of state, and I spend quite a number of nights alone. I sleep with the lights on in the bedroom or with a night light on.

I have made some friends here in Ontonogon. One of them claims to be a psychic. She has witnessed many strange ghostly appearances herself and is the bartender at the Candlelight Supper Club. She told me to tell the ghost to leave me alone and to "move on." So I did. Repeatedly. It seems to have solved the problem. Doors no longer slam shut or mysteriously open. No more loud and intense banging against the front door. No more feelings of a presence. Nothing brushes and moves the hair along my face while I watch television. It's quite a relief.

I used to be a legal assistant while living in Illinois, and I've done some writing on the side. Also, I've visited another haunted house.

On Steeplechase Road in Barrington Hills, Illinois, there is an extremely haunted old French manor house. About fifteen years ago, a family was murdered there. Their horses were also shot. They were tortured before they were killed, and, since then, their house seems to be on the weird side. A couple of years ago, a skeleton was dug up from the front yard beneath the big stone silo.

At the time, my husband worked for a private animal relocation firm out of Arlington Heights. They were contracted by the owner of the property to remove a wall full of bees that had to go. The bees had to be removed at night.

Tim, my husband, and his boss and another co-worker went there and removed the bees late one night, as directed, but the entire evening they had felt they were being watched. After the job was done, they sat around a huge stone fireplace in the living room and talked about what they felt. Tim and his boss knew I was interested in ghosts and called me to go there and see what I thought.

So, the following night, as Tim was on clean-up after the bee project, I accompanied him. No one lived in the house at the time. It had a gravel driveway about a third of a mile long. Tim and I pulled in and stopped the car before a towering manor. Instantly, a pickup with its headlights on bright pulled up behind us. Tim and I got out, and Tim walked back to the truck. He saw that an old man was the driver. Tim explained what we were doing there. The old man looked at him, smiling, and said, "Have fun!" Tim walked back to our car, and I asked him what had transpired. In that moment, the truck disappeared. It was just gone, vanished. There wasn't even any gravel dust.

As for the house, it had beautiful French windows, French doors, and oak floors. Twisting stone hallways were unusual, and an attached silo had a twisting spiral staircase. There were huge blood stains by the fireplace. The room above the kitchen had human teeth marks along the edges of the windows as if someone tried to chew his or her way with hands tied.

Bare bathroom showers were blood stained, and the curtains were torn down. While we were there, the power went out, so we walked through the constricting, twisting stone corridors to the silo room and up the long, spiral staircase guided only by the solemn beam of our flashlight. We stopped at the first level and looked down across the property through the narrow eye-slit windows.

We then continued to climb until we reached the top. Up there we found two bedrooms. One was huge. Tim cast the light into the room across from it, and the beam revealed some furniture. As he did this, I had my back to the open door of the other room just behind me. And something came up and stood pressing up against me and breathing on my neck.

I was so frozen with horror that I couldn't even move. I couldn't speak. I dreaded walking back down that horrible staircase and through the stone hallway to the living room then out the front door or even across the lawn with the towering steeples staring at me.

Even as I stood there laboring over the seemingly impossible journey back to safety, I grabbed Tim and told him only that I wanted to leave, that we *had* to leave. Down into the watery black space of hell we stepped. We passed the eerie bathrooms, stepped over the red stain near the fire pokers of the huge fireplace, passed the big, yellow-toothed piano and, at last, stepped out the front door.

The tower loomed over us, seemingly staring at us all the way to the car. I didn't feel free until Tim had driven the length of the gravel drive.

We returned to the lonely place during the benefit of daylight. We found what looked like a burial site beneath the silo. I even laid on it, and it was the right proportion for a body. Months later, a skeleton was actually dug up there.

In any event, the place was very haunted. A neighbor across the street reported seeing a little boy looking out one of the upper windows late at night.

ROSCOE THE PLAYFUL POLTERGEIST

Kristine Wiltzius, former owner of Back Bay Inn on Lake Shishebogama, had the unique opportunity to experience firsthand what affectionately became known as the resort's resident ghost. She was never one to believe in such things, but it wasn't long after purchasing Back Bay Inn that she began to wonder about the possible existence of specters.

At first, strange, unexplainable things began to occur. Kristine had a bar manager, Jeff, who lived on the premises and used to stay in the bar after closing to watch TV and unwind. One morning he came to her office and announced that he was going to buy a television for his living quarters. Kristine asked, "Why waste your money when there is a TV right in the bar you can watch." He then related the strange occurrences that were happening almost nightly in that popular Minocqua, Wisconsin, resort.

"After work, I have a regular routine for closing up. I check to make sure everyone is out of the building, and I lock the doors. Then I go into the bathrooms and turn off the lights, head to the kitchen and turn off the radio that the chef leaves on and shut off all the lights in the main room except one in the bar. About a week ago, while watching TV at the bar, I stood up to go behind the bar and get a soda, and I noticed that the light in the kitchen was on. I could have sworn I had shut it off. So, I went back and turned it off again. About half an hour later, the radio in the kitchen suddenly came on. I snuck back into the kitchen to see if someone was there, but there was no one. I figured that Dave, the chef, was playing tricks on me. I turned off the radio and made the rounds again, but I found nothing."

Jeff said these things continued to occur. Doors would open by themselves, lights would come on, and when the radio would turn on, it would be tuned to a different station than before. Jeff said he was too spooked to stay in the bar by himself anymore. He ended up buying a TV and quickly going to his quarters after work.

Kristine was skeptical about the whole thing. Then, one day the cleaning girl, Ardie, came running to her saying that she was afraid to be in the motel by herself. When Kristine asked her why, she told her, "I was cleaning room eleven and had just finished everything, but I was short one hand towel. As usual, I locked the room before going down to the maid's closet to get the towel. When I came back, the bed had an imprint of a person right in the middle of the bedspread, and I had just finished making the bed about two minutes before. Nobody could have gotten in there. Your motel is haunted."

Now Kristine was really beginning to wonder about ghosts. She managed to convince Ardie that the ghost was friendly and not to be afraid of it, but she wasn't so sure of that.

As time passed and more ghostly happenings were experienced by the staff, everyone just accepted the fact that the resort had a playful ghost on the premises. One of their best customers, Bob Ahlm, would stay at the resort about ten or twelve times a year. He had some friends up with him one time. His friends were put up in a room with two double beds. These people were avid fishermen and didn't frequent the bar the way Bob did, but one afternoon they came in to report that they had seen a ghost in their room. As the story went, about 2:00 A.M. they were both asleep when one man was suddenly jolted awake. He opened his eyes to see someone sitting at the foot of his bed. Thinking it was his friend, he said, "What's the matter? Can't you sleep?" The person didn't answer but stood up and walked toward the wall. Then he noticed that his friend was still in the next bed asleep. He yelled, and his friend woke up, and they both witnessed the man walk through the wall and disappear.

It was then that Kristine began telling them of all the strange things the staff had experienced. Bob decided the ghost needed a name, and he began to refer to him as Roscoe. From then on, everyone called him that.

Kristine's sister Nancy and her fiance, Alan, were visiting her for her birthday in August 1989. They decided to go back to the motel room. As they were approaching the room, Alan saw a white figure in the window of the room where they were staying. He said it looked out the window as they approached. The figure turned and floated away from the door toward the wall as they ran in but no one was there when they arrived. Alan was very nervous and never came back to visit again.

Over the ensuing months and years, Roscoe kept the staff entertained with his shenanigans. One day two guys were working on remodeling a cabin bathroom. As they were installing a shower surround, they realized they were short some tools they needed. One man said, "How will we keep the surround from falling out while we're gone?" The other took the screwdriver and nailed it to a support board with the hammer. That kept the stall in place. The men headed for the tools they needed. About five minutes later, when they returned, the screwdriver was gone. Each of the workers accused the other of taking the screwdriver, and both adamantly denied it. Later, one of them noticed the screwdriver lying on the window sill behind the curtain. Neither of them had put it there.

An employee, Pat, had the most encounters with Roscoe. Many days in the off season, she would help Kristine by painting the interiors of the cabins. When she worked, she liked to listen to a particular radio station. She was constantly annoyed because the radio would change stations by itself, or her cigarettes would disappear only to show up later in a drawer of a room she hadn't been in yet that day. Often when she was cleaning rooms, Roscoe would repeatedly slam the bathroom door of the room where she worked. When she would get sick of that, she would tell Roscoe to knock it off. Without fail the pranks would stop. She told of one time after cleaning an ashtray and replacing it on the nightstand, she turned to plug in the vacuum, and when she turned back, the ashtray was gone. She told Roscoe to give it back, but he ignored her. She started vacuuming. Later she turned around and the night-stand drawer was open, and the ashtray was in it. Nearly every day she would have another Roscoe prank to report.

Ardie and Pat had many more experiences with Roscoe. They were both waitressing one Friday night, and Ardie became very distressed because her special pen had disappeared. She questioned all the other employees, and no one knew what had happened to it. Pat said she had last seen it on the counter in the waitress station. About a month later, Pat was standing in the middle of the waitress station, taking a breather, when suddenly something dropped out of thin air at her feet. She picked it up and immediately recognized the cap of Ardie's pen. She returned it to Ardie, who asked Roscoe to please return the rest of her pen. About an hour later, Pat found the rest of the pen lying on the counter right where she had seen it last, before it disappeared.

Clearly Roscoe loved to take things and keep them awhile before returning them. The chef had many things disappear, only to have them reappear later quite mysteriously. He kept a pot scrubber on the shelf above the sink that he used frequently. One night he used it and put it back in the bowl on the shelf. Later when he went to use it again, it was gone. He searched everywhere to no avail. At the end of the night, he was cleaning up, and there it was back in its place on the shelf. The strangest theft occurred one Monday after a Sunday buffet. At the end of the night, the chef put the gravy in the walk-in cooler with the thought of using it on Monday for a special item on the menu. When he came in the next day, it was gone. He asked Kristine if it had been taken home by someone, and she said no. There was no one else around who could have taken it, so he took everything out of the cooler and literally tore the kitchen apart looking for that pan of gravy, but it was not found. Two days later, he came running from the kitchen and dragged Kristine back to the walk-in cooler. There was the pan of gravy right in the exact spot he had originally put it, and it hadn't been touched.

During the summer of 1991, Kristine had three students from the Milwaukee area working and living at Back Bay Inn. One of the guys had an American flag that he hung on the wall of his room. One day the flag disappeared. The student was really upset. About a week later, the students got off work and headed for their quarters. As one of them sat down on the couch, she noticed a big lump under the cushion. She stood up and lifted the cushion. There was the flag, folded up in perfect military fashion. Needless to say, the owner of the flag was elated to have it back.

Roscoe had a pension for neatness. Kristine would find clothing she had taken off and allowed to accumulate on the floor picked up and neatly folded under her pillow.

In September of 1991, Kristine was in the process of getting a divorce and was beginning to move her things from Back Bay Inn. She was going in and out of the office that was attached to the house when she noticed a huge black fly buzzing loudly against the widow. Every time she walked through there and saw the fly, she said, "Roscoe, why don't you kill that fly and get rid of it?"

A few minutes later, when she came through again, the buzzing had stopped, and the air reeked of bug spray. There had been a can of the stuff under the check-in desk, and Kristine went to look for it. Instead of its being in the back of the shelf, there was the can right in front and it had a wet ring of bug spray under it and down the side. The fly was gone.

Kristine's cat, Patches, even had an experience with Roscoe. One night she was sleeping soundly on the couch when suddenly she jumped straight up in the air about two feet and landed in a crouch with her fur straight up and her ears back. She growled. For a few minutes, she kept swatting at the air and growling before she jumped off the couch and hid under the bed.

One night before Kristine actually moved out, she was watching TV and noticed some movement out of the corner of her eye. She looked to her right and saw an eerie white form moving through the kitchen toward the back door. She was so stunned that she was unable to speak. The ghost stopped a moment and turned his head toward her, then continued to float right through the back door. Kristine knew she had finally been visited by Roscoe.

THE STEVENSON CREEK
CHIMNEY MYSTERY

A Chimney Where?

I first heard about the mysterious chimney in the woods from the bartender at George's Steak House, Barb Hegeman. I had not yet moved to Trout Lake and very rarely went to town. Barb reprimanded me for not having seen this true Northwoods icon, but I didn't give it a second thought at the time.

A few years later, I had moved to the north shore of Trout Lake, and I heard about the chimney again. Friends from the Milwaukee area knew about it. They came for a visit and took me to see the big stone chimney on the north shore of Stevenson Creek that feeds into Trout Lake. Standing alone like a silent sentinel, the three-story chimney looked like a bony finger of a buried giant in the earth.

We looked around the grounds for clues as to why such a huge chimney existed when so many other original structures in the Northwoods were far more modest. I later asked a neighbor on North Creek Road if he knew anything about the chimney in the woods. He said he thought

Looking northeast at the massive Stevenson log home.

the family moved away when their daughter got pregnant. He added that he seemed to remember that the lady of the house was very dainty. I even asked Paul Brenner, Boulder Junction's keeper of old photos and basic knowledge. He said he had a picture, but he couldn't find it.

Ever since I saw the old chimney, I felt a need to figure the mystery, understand what it had been all about. Leads came only slowly. About a year later, I received a letter from a friend with a phone number enclosed, suggesting I call on a woman in Sayner, that she might have a photograph of the old Stevenson Creek place.

I called, talked with a woman named Margaret, and she said that she did indeed have a picture of the house. I arranged to visit Margaret and Frank Maciejewski. Frank, as it turned out, worked in the CCC camp on White Sand Lake. In the CCC photo of him working in White Sand Creek, I saw the distinctive chimney. It was attached to a beautiful, big house.

I could see Palette Lake to the east of the location as there were hardly any trees after the loggers had come through that area. It was a strange and beautiful scene.

Frank said he had taken the picture about 1934 when they walked to the place one day from the CCC camp, which was northeast of the Stevenson Farm, as it was called then. Frank said whoever had lived in the place had already abandoned it by the time the photo had been taken. They had gone inside and found only some old bills and papers on the floor, no hint of its previous occupants or its builders or its purpose.

The Breakthrough

A caller on Wisconsin Public Radio during a Halloween show shed some light on the Stevenson Creek House Mystery. The caller, a Phil Barnard, said his dad was married to one of the Stevenson daughters. He said the family had moved to the Northwoods from Iona, Michigan, with the intention of starting a cranberry marsh near the Stevenson Creek area. That had been around the turn of the century. Then they moved to Ashland to open a store. The building was torn down prior to 1937, sold for lumber. The

Looking across Stevenson Creek north at the great home. This picture was taken in 1934. (Photo by Frank Maciejewski.)

father's name had been Arthur L. Stevenson and the family lived in the big house from about 1905 to 1911. The children were Ruth, Rolland, Raymond, and Esther. Across the creek from the house had been a lumber camp with a sawmill. There was also a railroad spur leading to the camp. The Stevenson farm originally covered some 2,500 acres, including a couple of lakes, most of which was sold for ten dollars an acre. The father, Arthur, died in 1938.

I asked Phil about photos, and he said he had some good ones. He promised to send copies.

From other avenues, I found out a bit more information. I ran into an older man who said the place "was a way station way back when. You should have seen the house. It was so well made that there was about three inches of crawl space under the floor for natural insulation." He said the family had planned to use Stevenson Creek in their cranberry operation by putting in a dam just west of the farmhouse.

Taken from the hill which leads in from the west to the Stevenson chimney. (Photo by Frank Maciejewski.)

Joanne Ohlsson of Boulder Junction filled in a few more details about the area surrounding the Stevenson house. Joanne said the big lumber mill across the creek lay where the North Trout Lake nature trail is today just west of Highway M and across the highway from where the road enters the Stevenson property. "That was the biggest lumber mill in the area," she said. "I remember digging up old bottles from the area. There's even a big wheel there for moving logs buried in the swamp." The rail line touched that mill in a north-south direction on that side of the roadway.

I also spoke with Pat Stocker, whose mom had been the postmaster's wife in Woodruff. They had visited the Stevenson chimney many times. "Mom has a painting of the house," she told me. I heard say the place was built to be a cranberry farm or something. Heck, it wasn't. The real reason they moved remains a mystery." That fit with the folklore about the place.

A Conversation with Phil Barnard

Knowing some of the history of the Stevenson-Barnard family involvement with the mystery house on Stevenson Creek in Boulder Junction answers a good many questions about the old chimney. The one haunting thing about the structure was why it was so big. Why did Arthur Stevenson build such a magnificent three-story home in the wilderness when, surely, a much simpler house would have been sufficient, especially in 1905, when much of the area was in its early settlement.

Barnard, who was seventy-three at the time of the taping, shared what he knew. "The Stevenson family lived in Ionia, Michigan, prior to 1890. My great-grandfather, F. W. Stevenson, owned a dry-goods store there. My granddad apparently didn't get along with F. W. — you know, fathers and sons some times don't get along.

"F. W. originally hailed from Madeline Island on Lake Superior. I have an old photo of my mom (Ruth) on the shore of Madeline Island with logs in the photo. I think those were from a loggers' lake drive. It was near the end of the the great logging era in the Northwoods, and I believe this is the main reason the family decided to move from the Ashland, Wisconsin, area to Boulder Junction.

"Arthur Stevenson and his wife and kids moved to the creek area just east of Trout Lake to begin a cranberry venture there. He bought a lot of land there and began.

"In 1936, I wanted to explore the old family home on Stevenson Creek. My dad told me it was off Highway M, but I couldn't find the dam from the cranberry marsh. I did find six beaver dams in the creek. There was one giant beaver lodge at the widest part of the creek. I'll never forget how big it was. I wondered if that wide part might be spring fed.

"On the south side of the creek, across from the house (it was still standing in 1936), there was an old sawmill.

Still rock solid after all these years, the old chimney of the Stevenson family home generates streams of unanswered questions. (Photo courtesy Joe Diorio.)

And there was a spur line to it. The road bed went from there to Palette and Escanaba Lakes."

Trout Lake Barracks

I had been told that the sawmill was just west of Highway M in the east-north shore of Trout Lake on the same boggy location that is now the North Trout Nature Trail, a place I walk daily.

Phil said that there was the lumber camp barracks. "None were standing," Phil said, "but there were rotting out hulks, so to speak. My mom said they were still active at the time they lived there in 1910. Still working then. I remember seeing a totally rotted bunkhouse in 1936. The roof was in good shape, at least. I didn't see the sawmill then; it had long gone into the ground."

More Stevenson Family History

"My grandfather's full name was Arthur Lincoln Stevenson. He was born in 1865 in Ionia, Michigan. He died in 1935. Grandmother was Emma Nash, and she, too, was born in 1865 in Clarksville, Michigan, some twenty miles from Ionia. Her family was in the banking business. They were farmers, too, and on my grandpa's side, F. W. owned that dry-goods store.

Arthur then moved to Ashland. Rolland was their first child. My mom, Ruth, was second. She was born September 16, 1891, in Ashland. She died in 1976 at the age of eighty-four in St. Croix Falls, Wisconsin.

"Raymond was the third child. I have no dates on him or the youngest, Esther.

"My dad's full name was Wilbur Dean Barnard. He was born in Beatrice, Nebraska, on April 1, 1889. He died October 10, 1969, at the age of eighty. He died in a car accident in St. Croix Falls."

The old chimney stands at attention north of Stevenson Creek. (Photo courtesy Porter Dean, Jr.)

Love on Trout Lake

"My mom and dad met at Trout Lake. My granddad didn't approve of the match as he was from a money background and dad was a forester at the Trout Lake nursery. Granddad didn't think he had enough money to support mom.

"One funny thing. My dad, being from Nebraska, never saw many trees. He'd tell me that he'd often go to the river to see trees growing. He loved them. In fact, he went to the University of Nebraska to study trees. He didn't graduate, only completed three years.

"He loved trees and got a job in Wisconsin with the Forestry Department at the ranger station. The nursery there was marvelous, and he was part of it. There are red pines there that he planted in 1912-1913. I remember during my visit there in 1936 seeing how big they had grown then."

The Saga of the Cranberry Marsh

"The entire cranberry-marsh saga is unclear to me," Phil said. "My grandpa read somewhere that cranberry farming was a good way to make money. So he bought the 2,500 acres in and around what is now Stevenson Creek. The area was for the most part devoid of trees; the loggers had left the area almost barren.

"But, take a look at the area. It wasn't really suited for cranberry farming. Arthur left because he really didn't know enough about cranberries. They need flat land. The dam he built on the creek forced water up steep slopes. He needed land that drained properly. It was just the wrong area; the terrain was too irregular.

"Perhaps the biggest problem in running a cranberry operation was that he concentrated on building the biggest and best house in the Northwoods. He had this thing that looking like a success made one a success. Thus the big and beautiful three-story house was as remote as it was a showplace. Maybe he was vain. I don't think he made a dime on the venture and abandoned the house and the property. Perhaps it was 1915 when everything was abandoned. That's my guess.

The Death of the Stevenson House

After the Stevensons abandoned what truly was the most beautiful house in the Northwoods, the state bought the property—all 2,500 acres—for ten dollars an acre. They then owned a massive three-story house, and they didn't know what to do with it. It would have made an excellent bed-and-breakfast in this day and age, but then it was thought to be a source of problem, especially with kids visiting the place.

Phil said, "They (the state) didn't want campers there or visiting kids. The state tore down the place for its logs."

It is ironic that just a few miles up the road is one of the largest cranberry areas in the world. Those modern-day cranberry marsh owners live in beautiful houses that would make the Stevenson family proud.